CAPTURED BY THE BERSERKERS

LEE SAVINO

FREE BOOK

Get a secret Berserker book, Bred by the Berserkers (only to the awesomesauce fans on Lee's email list)
Go here to get started... https://geni.us/BredBerserker

CAPTURED BY THE BERSERKERS

She'll be our captive. Forever.

Long ago, a witch turned us into monsters. Our only hope is to wait for the woman who can lift the curse.

A century later, we find her. Willow. Our miracle. She's hidden away in an abbey full of orphans, while evil men plot to sell her as a bride.

We'll break her out. We'll set her free. And then she'll be our captive until she realizes we're meant to be.

Author's Note: This is a MFM full-length ménage romance. There are no M/M scenes, just TWO hot, dominant warriors who claim the same woman...

Remember to download your free book at www.leesavino.com

The Berserker Saga

Sold to the Berserkers
Mated to the Berserkers
Bred by the Berserkers (FREE novella only available at www.leesavino.com)
Taken by the Berserkers
Given to the Berserkers
Claimed by the Berserkers

Berserker Brides

Rescued by the Berserker
Captured by the Berserkers
Kidnapped by the Berserkers
Bonded to the Berserkers
Berserker Babies
Owned by the Berserkers
Night of the Berserkers
Tamed by the Berserkers
Mastered by the Berserkers - coming in 2020

WILLOW

The abbey lay on the hip of the curving road. I followed the path, hurrying to be sure I reached its large oak doors before the bell tolled for evening prayers. Whenever the friar sent me on an errand to the village, he gave me strict warnings to return before sunset. Tonight, I hurried not only to escape his punishment, but to outrun the almost-full moon. I needed to be hidden well away before it rose and brought the sickness upon me.

Lost in my thoughts, I startled when a shadow fell across my path.

"Good evening," a deep voice murmured, right at my back. I let out a shriek and dropped my basket.

Two large men stood on the edge of the path. Warriors, though they bore no weapons I could see. Both massive, with broad shoulders and great muscled arms, but, somehow, I hadn't noticed them standing there until they spoke. Even now, they seemed to blend with the sun-dappled forest as they loomed over me.

"Calm yourself, lass. I did not mean to scare you." One of

them, a redhead with hair to his shoulders, stooped and picked up my basket.

"You don't need to try to scare women, Leif," the second warrior grunted. "Your face scares them enough."

The redhead, Leif, didn't take his eyes from me.

"My apologies, lass." He spoke with a strange accent but a bit of a lilt I recognized from the Highlands, a mountainous area many leagues from the abbey.

Hands trembling, I took the basket and clutched it to my chest. The warriors' gaze swept up and down my form, lingering on my breasts. They kept their distance. If they made any move, I would drop my burden again and run to the abbey doors, a race no doubt I would lose.

"You're not too frightened?" Leif cocked his head to the side. He had an open, honest face, a scar marking his chin, and a full, lush mouth.

When I shook my head, he flashed an arrogant smile. "See, Brokk? She's a brave little thing. I wager it's your ugly face tying her tongue." He gave me a wink.

My cheeks heated.

"Don't embarrass her," Brokk muttered, the stern set of his mouth in contrast to his partner's cocky grin.

"And miss the pretty color in her cheeks? Like the bloom of a rose." When Leif smirked again, I caught a quick flash of fang. His canines curved over his lower teeth. "You're lovely, lass."

My lips parted. My heart fluttered like a bird caught in a briar.

The second warrior cleared his throat. He wasn't as handsome as his companion, but his blunt features and glowering brow had their own arresting charm. "Leif thinks he has a way with women. I will not let him keep you long,"

Brokk assured me, though at the word "keep" I took a step back.

With a low, soothing sound, the warriors hemmed me in. My head craned upwards to take in one stern, one smiling face.

I clutched my basket tighter. The warriors blocked my escape, but for some reason, I felt no fear. My body warmed further still, responding to the heat emanating from them.

"Can I help you, sirs?" I rasped. My dry throat worked to get the words out. Maybe, if I stayed polite, they would let me go.

"Do you live yonder?" Brokk nodded to the abbey, his voice gruff but kind.

"Yes, sir."

"What's your name?" Leif asked.

"It's Willow," I whispered.

"Willow." Leif rolled my name on his tongue, and I felt a prickle between my legs. My nipples throbbed.

"Willow," Brokk echoed, and his face softened a little.

The ache in my breasts increased, and wetness trickled from my nether lips.

Leif raised his head and drew in a deep breath. Both warriors pierced me with the look of a predator fixing on its intended prey. I swayed between them, caught in their bright-yellow gaze.

My desire blazed to life, followed by fear.

"I should not be here," I blurted. "I should not be talking to you." The friar warned me and my sister orphans against strange men. Whenever he caught one of us speaking to any in the village, all of us bore the punishment.

It would be night soon, complete with the dreaded full moon.

"I need to go," I whispered. "Please."

For a moment, I thought they would not let me leave, but then Leif stepped away, giving me a clear path to the abbey.

"Take care, Willow," Brokk said in his gentle rumble.

"We'll watch over you," Leif added. "Make sure you get safely to the door. After all, there are dangerous men about."

My heart dropped to my feet, and he winked at me again.

For a second, his eyes seem to pulse with a golden light. It faded, leaving an ordinary man. Ordinary except for the handsome face, the strapping neck, the fine muscles stretching the leather jerkin he wore.

With a small nod, I scrambled the rest of the way home.

∽

INSIDE, the wall propped me up as I pressed a hand over my breast, willing my heartbeat to slow. I'd never had such a response to a man before, not even to Joseph, the village blacksmith's apprentice who always smiled at me. I held my hands out and watched them tremble. Something about those warriors, the way they couldn't take their eyes off me... my body buzzed, blood roaring. I felt I'd waited all my life to meet those men.

What was happening to me? I should've asked the warriors where they'd come from, and their purpose. I should've done something besides stand there like a fool, my face flushed and my heart racing.

Light filtered through the colored window above me, staining my hands red. What a fool. My encounter meant nothing. Warriors on a journey had found brief entertainment frightening a scrawny girl. As soon as they laughed over the encounter, they'd forget me.

Me? I'd think about them, and my wicked, sinful flesh would burn for days. In cool darkness, I slipped along the stone floor and passed through the sanctuary, head bowed against the cold marble stares of the saints. I'd visited the sanctuary often enough I'd memorized their faces. Perfect, and high above me. A good girl would do penance on her knees for even speaking to such a pair of such fine men. As for the thoughts I'd had when trapped between their large strapping bodies...I could never do enough penance to atone.

On a whim, I set my basket down and approached the likeness of Mother Mary. The statue stood at the front altar, her expression serene and pure. When younger, I'd pretended she was my real mother. I'd prayed for answers, for relief from the sickness I'd endured since becoming a woman. The Church taught suffering purged the soul. Even my prayers were sinful, the desperate begging of a weak woman.

Why am I like this? How long must I suffer? I found no answers in the beautiful, carven face.

"Willow," a low voice called. A young woman crept from the shadows. Sage, my closest friend among all the orphans. She and I had been brought to the abbey around the same time. We shared a similar height and slim build. Despite my dark hair and her fair locks, we could have been sisters.

"Did you finish the errand?"

"Yes." I kept my voice down so it would not echo in the cavernous space. I'd asked the nuns once why the statues of the saints got to live in such a beautiful open area, while we shared beds in the dormitory. It took a few rounds of discipline before I understood the Church allowed luxury to the rich and the dead.

"Are you coming to Vespers?" she asked.

"No, I cannot. It is almost a full moon."

Sage nodded. She suffered the same sickness I did, though less frequently, while mine grew worse every month.

"Here." She handed me a handkerchief wrapped around a few oatcakes. The nuns did not allow us to eat if we did not go to prayers, but I had to hide away to suffer in silence when the moon rose.

"I still must visit the friar." I gestured to the basket I'd fetched for him.

Sage picked it up. "I will do it."

"He has been grumpy ever since Hazel disappeared."

"I'll be all right." Sage lifted her chin.

Without a word, I raised her sleeve and studied the bruises there. The marks came from a man's grip on her pale, thin arm. There would be more on her legs, but she would hate my pity more than she hated the friar's illicit touch.

I released her sleeve. "The shopkeeper gave us a fair price for the herbs. He wants more of the tincture you made for backaches."

With a tight smile on her lovely face, Sage nodded and slipped away. I prayed again, this time hoping the friar would be happy with the earnings she brought. The wool and weavings the orphans spun and the produce we harvested paid our way, though the friar always found a reason to complain about our cost to him. Only Sage could soothe him. He preferred young blonde things. God help the younger girls if he ever tired of Sage.

I scoffed at my own joke. I'd lived in the abbey long enough to know God did not help orphans.

A red sun sank in the sky as I hurried across the gardens, accompanied by the sweet singing of the nuns. A few years ago, I'd close my eyes and imagine my mother sang to me. A pretty dream, for she'd given me up almost as soon as she birthed me.

I slipped behind the mulberry bushes and picked the lock of an old shed. Inside, behind a few barrels used for dyeing cloth, Sage and I had wrapped a chain and set of shackles around a large rock. In a few minutes, I would bind myself there and wait for the fever to take my mind.

The shack sat back in the woods, near a gurgling brook, the forest sounds enough to cover the moans and cries escaping my throat when the fever reached its peak. No one should be out in the gardens this late, but, just in case, Sage would do her best to keep everyone away.

I set the oatcakes down, too nervous to eat. I should kneel and pray. Instead, I paced. During the next few hours, I would bind myself in such a way I would not be able to touch between my legs, but the ache would become unbearable, my mind tormented with dreams of hands upon my body, caressing my flesh. In the morning, Sage would come and free me from my fevered sleep.

My body already simmered, the excitement a result of speaking to the warriors earlier. The thought of them caused heat to burst through me, a throbbing warmth leaving a slight trickle of wetness between my legs. The first spark would turn into an ember and light the fire that would become a blazing inferno.

One day, I would have the courage to talk to a man and flirt with him as Leif had with me. We'd slip into the forest and press against each other, his large hands eager and possessive on my skin. Afterwards, we would lie together on the forest floor, curled as close as petals in a rosebud.

With a sigh, I picked up the shackles. The cold iron stung my hands.

A clink of metal on metal made me still. The sound

didn't come from the fetters I held, but from outside. Someone had found my hiding place.

I waited, holding my breath, but no one burst into the shack. The friar had become more surly and suspicious since our fellow orphan Hazel disappeared. She had just come into heat and had the courage to defy him. We assumed he'd sold her off to a husband, but no one knew for sure. The friar had struck Sage when she'd worked up the courage to ask.

Dusky light shone through the cracks in the shack. Twilight approached. If caught now, I could claim I'd been searching for the dye barrel. After setting the shackles down, I eased the door open, stepped into the dim evening, and froze.

Rank upon rank of giant warriors closed in on the abbey. They crept across the grounds without a sound. They all had weapons, axes or daggers worn at their belts. The dying light showed their hands to be free.

I gathered myself to scream. A rough palm closed over my mouth. I let out a muffled shriek.

"Hello, Willow," a voice rasped in my ear.

Disbelieving, I stilled. The voice and strong arms locked around me belonged to the redheaded warrior. His black-haired friend stood at his side, frowning.

"Get her out of here." Brokk jerked his head.

My protests muffled by Leif's large hand, I kicked and fought as much as I could, to no effect. The warrior swung me up, arms still clamped around me, and dragged me deeper into the woods.

"Stay calm now, lass." Red locks tickled my cheek as he whispered in my ear. "You're safe now. Danger is coming to the abbey, but we'll get your friends out."

Danger?

Why would battle-hardened warriors attack an abbey full of innocent women and girls? Had the friar cheated someone and incurred a lord's wrath?

Despite my struggles, the warrior carried me into the woods until the trees crowded my view of the abbey, its turret shining with the last light of day. I went limp against him, hoping he would let down his guard. Perhaps I could still escape to warn Sage. She would be in the dormitory now, reading to the little ones, or perhaps setting out a tankard of ale for the friar to drink, in hopes he'd get too drunk to bother her. Around midnight, she'd slip out to check on me. She wouldn't find me.

Of course, by then, she'd be taken, too.

Throat tight, I sobbed silently against Leif's hand.

"Shh, lass, it's all right." He set me down but kept me clamped against his broad chest. "You're in danger. You and the other spaewives. We've come to rescue you."

I let my eyes close and legs sag as if I'd fainted. Leif propped me up, but when he tried to turn me into a less awkward hold, I broke from his arms.

After a few steps, he caught me fast. I went crazy, flailing in an attempt to get free. Not for myself. They'd captured me, but if I could get close enough to the abbey and scream loud enough to warn Sage and the others...

"Oh, no, you don't," Leif grunted, lifting me again. His large hand closed around my throat. He squeezed in warning, and though he did not cut off my air, his grip silenced me. Brokk hovered close.

"Put her down. Quickly. Bind her. We cannot risk her warning any guards who might be about."

"Stay calm." Leif shook me. "You're in no danger as long as you obey." He pinned me belly down on the forest floor, holding my wrists at the small of my back. Before I could scream, Brokk jammed something into my mouth.

"This isn't going the way I wanted," Leif muttered.

I panted and cried as they finished binding me. Then Leif sat back with me in his arms.

"There, now. Safe and secure."

I glared at him, trying to push the bitter-tasting leather from my mouth. A growl sounded in my throat. False bravado—the rest of me shook.

"You going to fight me, Willow?" The warrior teased my hair from my face with surprising gentleness. I thrashed, throwing off his touch.

"Stop," Brokk ordered, squatting close. His command stilled me. "We will not allow you to hurt yourself." The sharpness in his tone and gaze warned me to behave.

"We're not here to harm you," Leif repeated.

I blinked at them. I sat trussed and gagged and trembling. A young maiden captured in the woods by two warriors. Limbs numb, skin covered in goose bumps. My light summer dress provided no protection from a chill in the air strange for a late summer night.

"You'll want to know why we are here," Leif interpreted. "Fear not. It'll all be brought to light."

A scream shattered the still air. It came from the abbey.

"Damn, damn." Leif hauled me up.

"Go to the meeting place. I'll catch up," Brokk told him, and ran back to join the other warriors.

I dug my heels into the dirt, but Leif hauled me over his shoulder. His large hand smacked my bottom when I struggled again.

"None of that now," he said. I went limp again, the fight truly gone out of me this time. Straining to raise my head, I could only watch as Brokk and his fearsome comrades advanced to attack my home.

∼

LEIF CARRIED ME EASILY, striding in silence through the woods. His pace picked up to a trot when we came to a field. We traveled far beyond where I'd ever roamed. Sage and I had often talked about running away but had never gone much beyond the shack we'd made our hiding place.

The last light glimmered through the trees when the warrior set me down again. I watched him through the screen of my hair.

"Water?" He offered me a little waterskin tied to his belt.

I shook my head.

"More for me." He drained the skin, his beautiful throat working as he swallowed.

When he moved to touch me, I flung myself back with enough violence to leave furrows on the ground.

"Shh, shh," he soothed. "I'll untie the gag." He held his hands up as if trying to coax a wild creature. "Do I have your word you will not scream?"

I stared at him. His words grazed my overwrought brain. I was captive and bound several miles from my home, and at this warrior's mercy.

Leif knelt in front of me.

"You will not scream," he told me. "If you do, there will be consequences. I might like the consequences, but I promise you will not. Besides"—his tone gentled—"even if you do cry out, there is no one around to hear you. And no one will take you from me." For a moment, his gaze darkened. I wanted to huddle into a tight ball.

Instead, I let him take off the gag then I spat in his face. He drew back, blinking in surprise.

"You coward," I said. "Do you like kidnapping innocent girls?"

He wiped at his speckled cheek.

"Oh, aye," he said with a grin. He didn't seem upset, more amused by my anger.

"Let me go," I ground out, struggling against my bonds. I had to do something. This warrior loomed over me, three times my size, and all of it muscle. He'd promised not to hurt me, but I'd have to be a fool to trust him—wouldn't I?

"I'll free you," he went on, "when I can be sure you will not run."

I turned my head away for a moment. I wasn't afraid, not of him. My cheeks flushed, my body heated from his closeness. Under the thin fabric of my shift, my breasts felt heavy and swollen, and I wished I could bare them to the night air.

When I met the warrior's gaze, a jolt went through me. I closed my eyes, but too late to hide the hunger in them.

This time, when he brushed the hair from my face, I did not fight.

"What do you want with me?" Even to me my voice sounded low and husky.

His golden eyes drank me in. His thumb rubbed my lower lip. "Everything," he murmured. "I want everything you have to give, and more."

LEIF

My little captive glared up at me, a furrow on her brow. Her frown did nothing to mar her beauty. Her dark hair framed her lovely face, her limbs and curved body smooth and pleasing, but her temper had me hard as a rock.

"Everything you have to give," I told her. She could not know what I meant, of course. But I couldn't help speak the truth. Her journey to full surrender had begun the moment she came into our possession. The sooner she understood, the easier it would be.

Our friend Knut had briefed Brokk and me on what it would be like when we took a mate.

"You need to woo her," the gruff warrior told us. "Say soft, sweet things. Be gentle."

But, in the heat of the rescue, the beast had surged forth, our baser nature battling to assert itself and claim her. Even now, I struggled to keep from throwing her to the ground and burying my cock inside her. The beast wanted to mark our woman, to bond her to us before we brought her back to the pack home. If she didn't bond to us before then, the Alphas might not allow us to keep her...

Steady, brother. Brokk linked to my mind. *You must keep control.*

I bit back my retort. Brokk was right. His stern grip on the beast kept me sane all these years.

Are you so sure she is the one for us? he asked, the tinge of hopefulness in his tone keeping me from snarling my answer.

In my mind's eye, I saw the scene before him. Brokk lingered near the shed where we had found our precious captive, watching the Berserkers carry off their chosen women. Some of the females came quietly, tucked into their captors' arms. Others wept as the Berserkers led them away. A rare few fought, their struggles quickly overcome by the massive warriors.

There are many women to choose from, Brokk observed.

You know as well as I her scent called to us. And her courage, hiding under the false meekness. This girl is strong.

Find out more about her. Brokk severed our connection before I could answer. I didn't let his rudeness ruffle me. My warrior brother and I had disagreed many times over the years, and most of the arguments I had won. Soon, he would share my confidence Willow belonged to us. Always careful, he wanted to be sure we'd found the right mate.

Mates are for life, he reminded me. *We must be sure we choose the right one.*

And we want a strong one. One able to bear sons, I told him. *Sons, and a few red-haired daughters to make me gray.*

His grudging chuckle echoed in the bond between our minds, satisfying me.

The girl still sat on the forest floor, her head cocked to the side as she watched me.

I drew my knife, and she blanched.

"Easy, lass." I fell into the Highlander lilt. Brokk and I and most of the Berserkers hailed from the North Lands, but after we'd settled on the island, I'd found I preferred the speech pattern of the mountain men. Once I cut the leather ties we used to bind her, Willow relaxed. I took her arms and chafed her wrists, clucking over the red marks.

"If ye had not fought, we would not have tied ye." I turned her hand and placed a quick kiss over her pulse. "Of course, if ye had not fought, I'd have a harder time convincing Brokk to choose ye."

"Choose me?"

"Aye," I said. "To be our mate."

She shrank in on herself, paling under her freckles. I did not like her terrified expression.

"Do not fear," I soothed, even as my beast fought for dominance, surging to the fore to protect the frightened woman. "Brokk and I will care for you. Even now, he's wondering what makes me so sure we can bond...but I know you have the strength to be our bride."

I held out the waterskin, a peace offering. When she took it, my fingers touched hers. The air filled with her scent.

"Brokk will tease me for making camp so soon, but I want to get some food into you and give you a chance to know us better before we continue our journey. Something in you calls to us. You feel it, too, aye?"

She pressed her lips together.

"Stubborn. No need for you to talk. I can smell the truth."

Ducking her head, she tried to hide her blush.

She's almost in heat, I observed to Brokk. *I wonder if she knows it.*

Ask her.

I opened my mouth and got hit in the face with the waterskin. By the time I'd scrambled to my feet, my little captive had found hers and raced into the thick woods.

WILLOW

Heartbeat pounding in my ears, I crashed through the forest. Behind me, the redheaded warrior snarled, and I darted into the thick brush, barefoot. The friar didn't like to spend money on things for the orphans, and my feet became calloused from going without shoes every summer. I'd longed to run these woods. A few months before Hazel disappeared, she and Sage and I had started racing one another, practicing for the day we would escape.

"Bad idea, lass," the warrior growled down my neck. I shrieked and dodged around a tree, ducking under brambles. I heard Leif cursing and the rending of fabric. I'd better get away, for, now, the punishment he promised me would be more severe.

My course zigzagged through the forest until I burst out onto a wagon road. My feet pounded down the path, stopping short when I came to a crossroads. One way would take me to the abbey. I could go back and warn my friends before being captured again. Or I could continue and see how long I could remain free.

I hesitated.

"Got you now." The warrior pounced. We tussled. He took me to the ground then tossed me over his shoulder once again.

Frantic, I bit him until I tasted blood.

"Stop." He gave my bottom a jarring slap that reverberated all the way through me. I shrieked, and the place between my legs pulsed.

"That's right," he said, squeezing my bottom cheek with a firm grip. "I've got more swats for you, if you don't behave. You went against your word."

I struggled, and he set me down, hard enough to knock the breath from my lungs.

"You will learn." He wrapped the leather ties around my wrists again.

"Oh, please," I blurted.

"Now you beg?" He bound my hands before me and looped a leather thong around my neck before fisting it tight in his hands. He gave it a tug.

"Please don't do this." My cheeks heated. Bound, humiliated, I felt excitement stirring in my loins. The moon rose in the deepening sky. My heat would soon be upon me. I had to get away. "I'll be good."

"Aye, you will. Leashed and collared at my side." He drew me forward by the leather lead, handsome features sharp and stern. "I'll train you to be at my beck and call, and thank me for the privilege."

"I'll go with you." I caught the tether between us. "Please just tell me if my friends are safe."

He blinked.

"Aye, lass," he said. "They are safe. Do not worry. The pack will watch over them."

I closed my eyes. "Then I will go with you and do as you say." *For now.*

A pause, and I opened my eyes to find the warrior studying the tether around my neck. He took a silver arm ring from around his bicep, bent the metal to open it and again to close it around my throat. The silver cooled my skin, but the rest of me flushed, tingles running through me at his touch and attention.

"There." He undid the lead and fixed it to the metal instead. A collar and a leash, like a dog. And my traitorous body grew excited.

My hands curled into fists, but even if I could best such a warrior, I couldn't fight him and my desires at the same time.

Leif stepped back with a smirk.

My jaw clenched. "How long, then, am I to remain your captive?"

He drew me forward, though I dug in my heels. "Forever." He cocked his head to the side.

I bit my lip. I would bide my time and plan my escape.

"Come, lass."

As he led me forward, I glanced back but could not glimpse the abbey tower at all. Funny how often I'd dreamed of leaving, and now a warrior dragged me away.

"From one slavery to another," I muttered.

"Mate, not slave," Leif corrected. "Brokk wonders why my beast chose you, but it's plain to me. You're a courageous lass."

I jerked my head no, and he grinned. "Sure you are. You've got enough fight to face us." He dipped his head close to mine. "I like it when you fight." He chucked me under the chin before stepping back and tugging on the lead. "Now. We march."

I followed him. He stopped and started a few times, as if testing me. I thought about pulling away but remained, as obedient as I'd promised. I would wait for my opportunity to escape.

I licked my lips several times before daring to speak. "Where are you taking me?"

"Back to the pack home on the mountain," he told me. "Though tonight we will spend on our own in the woods."

Dark settled over us. The moon started its ascent.

"Why were you out alone in that shed?" he asked.

"Hiding from the nuns and the friar." Before he could ask why, I continued. "What will you do with them?"

"The holy man and women?"

"Yes."

"Some of the nuns are spaewives, also. The Berserkers will take them captive. The rest will be set free, unless they are found guilty of mistreating you and the others. If so, they will be punished. Perhaps even destroyed."

I stumbled, and he caught my arm, holding it until I jerked away.

"And the friar?" He had mistreated many of us.

In the darkness, his eyes glowed. "We shall see." His tone turned dark. "Are you worried about his fate?"

"I worry about mine," I answered, "and the fate of my sister orphans."

"Have no fear for them. They are safe now—forever."

"As slaves."

He stopped in his tracks and turned, towering over me. I took a step back.

"Mark my words, lass. They are safer now than they've ever been. They might be frightened, tonight, but the warriors who claim them will see to their every need."

A prickle of heat curled through me. "How can you say that? You came in the night and took us from our home."

"And yet I do not smell any fear," he said. "Your scent cannot lie. It tells me you are...eager."

I flushed, wishing I could hide from his intense gaze. Again, my body had betrayed me.

With a finger, he raised my chin. "It's nothing to be ashamed of, lass. You're ready for your mates and want us. Soon, your heat will claim you."

"How did you know?" I licked my lips, glancing again at the moon.

"How often does it come on you? The fever."

"Once a month."

"So you chain yourself in the shed."

I nodded. "I have to. Another girl, she got free. The friar had to go into the village after her. He punished all of us, and we never saw her again." Or Hazel, who disappeared soon after telling us the friar had done away with the lust-filled girl.

BROKK

She's fighting it, Leif said into my mind. I raised my head. Darkness had fallen over the abbey; only one window held light. A few Berserkers lingered, checking for stray spaewives. They'd tied the remaining nuns up and would stand guard over them all night, setting them free in the morning. We had the night to get our mates back to the mountain.

She is already consumed by the mating heat, but it may take longer to convince her she's ours.

We don't have time for games. You think she's our mate, you deal with her. You have a silver tongue, Leif. Use it.

Silence. The past few seasons, Leif and I had been more and more at odds, our beasts provoking us to anger. A mate would soothe both our tempers. She'd have to. If Leif's beast or mine broke free, neither of us would survive.

We must return to the mountain. I tried reasoning with my warrior brother. *The mage who gathered all the women here might be coming for them.*

She is afraid. The holy man who watched over the spaewives punished them for going into heat. That's why she hid.

Anger flared up in me. *The holy man remains at the abbey. Rolf and Thorbjorn are still questioning him. Let me ask them if this is true.*

Thorbjorn's response came choked with rage.

It's worse, I reported to Leif. *The holy man mistreated some of his wards and used them then sold them to the Corpse King.*

For a moment, we struggled to contain our raging beasts. Fur sprouted along my arms as I started to complete the Change.

Leif sent me a lingering impression—the woman Willow standing bound tight at his side. So small and brave, her chin up and back straight, she let Leif guide her through the darkening night.

We will protect her, Leif said. *She is safe beside me. She will forget her fear as we train her to our touch.*

My beast calmed. Though I still burned at the thought of any man putting his hands on our woman without her permission, I knew Leif would protect her.

The friar is close to breathing his last, I told Leif. *Even now, I hear his shouts and pleas for mercy. Rolf and Thorbjorn will show him none.*

A moment later, the cries stopped.

Brokk, a deep voice called to me.

Thorbjorn, I answered. *Do you have them all out?*

All but one small blonde slip of a girl. Her name is Sage. The warmth in his tone told me he was already smitten.

Be sure to claim her as yours before you return to the mountain. Grinning, I was trotting back to the woods when a rotten scent reached my nose.

I stopped in my tracks and went to the garden wall.

A faint mist crept up the road ahead of a hundred lurching shapes.

Draugr. The Corpse King's servants came for our women. I linked to the pack.

The enemy is coming. Get out now!

WILLOW

While the warrior worked to light a fire, I huddled next to him, arms bound and legs hobbled. Even though he'd tied me up, he had seen to my comfort, laying out a bedroll out for me to sit on and producing a few oatcakes from his pack, as well as a silky wolf pelt.

The chill had dissipated, leaving the night warm and fine, yet I shivered. Not with cold. The moon rose, and soon the fever would take me. I would be helpless in its clutches, my loins throbbing, sweat trickling down my brow as I moaned for relief...

"Easy, lass," Leif said without looking up. "I can smell your excitement from here."

Pressing my legs together, I let out a little whimper. "Will you not let me go?"

He met my eyes a moment. All hope died in me at the hunger burning there. I sagged in my bonds. Soon I would not be able to beg him to free me. The desire in my body would match his, taking over my mind, consuming my very soul. How many nights had I dreamt of a man like him come to sate me? He'd find me in the darkness, his touch gentle and strong. Everything about his hard-muscled form would satisfy. We'd lie together, each touch a secret promise too precious for our mouths to utter. Morning would find us twined together, me safe in his arms.

My sigh came out a little moan.

When I raised my head again, the warrior's eyes burned gold.

"Keep it up, lass, and I'll have you on your back in a second. See if I don't. We made an oath not to touch you until you were ready, but there's only so much a man can take."

I tucked my head down, struggling to keep everything inside, even as a trickle of wetness ran down my leg.

"It's not my fault," I whispered. But the moon rose higher. When the heat came upon me, how would I explain?

"Brokk better get back soon," the warrior muttered, and continued to feed the fire. He cut a handsome figure in the low light, the finest-looking man I'd ever seen. Long legs, broad shoulders, profile sharp and elegant.

I licked my lips. "You made an oath?"

"Aye." A muscle jumped in his cheek. "We all did."

He rose, and I noted the outline of his member straining against his breeches.

The warrior cleared his throat, and I forced my gaze up. "What do you want with me?"

Leif parted his lips as if to answer then snapped his head to the right. A second later, he leapt to his feet, kicking the fire out.

"Come, lass." He slashed my bonds and drew me up.

"What is it?"

"The enemy." Smoke plumed from the dying blaze, and the contents of his pack lay scattered about, but Leif did not stop. He pushed me ahead of him, plunging us both into the forest. I cried out as branches tore at my arms, but he didn't slow.

"What enemy?"

Leif led me to the road. I heard it then—hissing. I wrinkled my nose at the stench of rotting flesh.

"The Corpse King." Leif pulled me across the road at a run. "He is coming for you."

LEIF

They're here, I sent to Brokk. *The draugr. I sense them coming up the road.*

Brokk cursed. *They're at my back, as well. We are surrounded.*

I pulled the woman into a crouch behind a boulder. With our escape cut off, we had to find a place to hide. How did they get here so fast?

The area must be under watch. No matter. We must find a way to get Willow out.

Not going to fight me on whether or not she's our mate? I joked, but Brokk responded, blunt and serious as usual.

Later. When there is time.

I did not argue. I shouldn't be surprised Brokk put up resistance towards our newfound mate, even though it had been a long time since we'd had a woman.

"What—" Willow started, and I clamped a hand on her mouth.

"Silence. Something's coming."

The hiding place I'd chosen gave me a view of the road. Mist swept up the ancient path, strange for such a warm, fine night. I muttered a curse. The Corpse King had spells to control the weather.

I forced her head against my chest. "Be very quiet, lass. I know you don't trust me, but there's evil in this world beyond your ken, and I'll do my best to shield you from it."

Instead of resisting, she shuffled closer to me. She tucked her head down, and I stroked her hair to soothe her.

Another minute passed, and the fog on the road thickened. The hissing grew louder. Whatever came towards us seemed to fly past, faster than I'd known Grey Men to move.

Chills crawled up and down my skin.

"Down, lass." I pushed Willow to the ground and covered her with my body. The air over my back grew cold. I choked on the thick, rotten stench. Above our heads, the trees creaked, straining under the tainted wind. The beast in me pushed to the fore, ready to fight against the evil sweeping over us.

I waited until the wind died and the forest stilled once more.

"All right. It's passed."

At my side, Willow panted, her heartbeat a frightened tattoo.

"What was that thing?"

"I do not know," I told her. "The Corpse King has much power."

"All right." Her teeth clacked together in the sudden cold. I wished for the pelt to toss around her shoulders, but I'd left it in my haste to escape. How foolish to think us safe enough to stop for the night.

My hand brushed the woman's hair back from her face. If I focused, I could almost sense the path of her blood through her body, running sweet and free as a river to the sea. If I put my mouth on her throat, her pulse would flutter under my tongue, inviting the prick of my fangs.

My spine tingled, my limbs prickling with the magic of the Change. Rage filled me, white hot and delicious, a flow of tainted power transforming me into a beast strong enough to rip apart the draugr—and more. I blinked, and my vision turned red. A new enemy in the grove with us—tearing and clawing to escape the cage of my mind.

Brokk. I reached to him. *I need you.* We'd spent over a century aiding each other in restraining our beasts. He knew what would happen if my beast took hold, and would not refuse me, even if we disagreed over taking a mate.

I'm coming, brother. I sensed him crashing through the forest, desperate to get to me in time. *Hang on. Don't lose control.*

I dug my nails into my palms, feeling the prick as they turned into razor-like claws. Over a hundred years waiting for the woman who could lift the curse, and now that she sat here by my side, it may be too late.

WILLOW

"Stay here," Leif growled and leapt to his feet. He tied my tether to a small tree. "And keep quiet, no matter what evil you see."

"Wait," I cried. Something changed. His form was hunched and rigid, every muscle tensed. "Are you going to fight them?"

He paused with his back to me. "Frightened for me, lass?" His rough guttural voice was tempered with a touch of teasing.

I hugged my knees to my chest. I should want to escape this warrior, but I did not want him to leave.

"Do not fear, little captive. I will scout the area and return. If you remain here, I can keep you safe." He vanished into the forest.

Alone, I sat in a shroud of silence. The normal night sounds—the creaking of insects, the hoot of an owl—receded. Dread hung in the air.

Darkness pressing on me, I waited, huddled where the warrior had put me. I could escape if I undid the tether, but my instincts told me to stay still. Even if I ran, the warrior would track me down, and he seemed more dangerous than any other enemy, even the Corpse King he'd spoken of.

A shadow moved by my side. Jerking up, I screamed, but a hard hand slapped over my mouth, muffling the sound.

"Quiet," a voice muttered in my ear. Brokk.

I sagged against him, almost sobbing with relief. His scent filled my lungs, fresh and tantalizing. Pressed against his hard chest, my body remembered its arousal.

He dropped his pack on the ground and examined my tether.

"Leif is gone," I whispered.

Undoing my lead from the tree, he hunkered down, pulling me with him under the shelter of a hemlock. I obeyed, holding my breath.

Unlike the redheaded warrior, Brokk offered no kind word, no reassuring touch. These men had captured me, yet I expected comfort from them. Leif made it clear I tempted him. Brokk didn't seem to like me.

Still, I shifted close to him, feeling safer by his side.

"It's so quiet," I whispered after a few heavy minutes. "There are no birds."

"They sense the presence of evil," Brokk replied.

"Something came up the road," I whimpered. "I couldn't see because Leif covered me, but I felt it. He said it's coming for me." My voice died in a frightened squeak.

"I know, Willow." His tone remained stern, but he tugged the lead, drawing me to a kneeling position at his side. I relaxed in the shelter of his great body.

"It's after me?"

"Yes. Hush."

We waited in silence until Leif slipped in beside us.

"You got the bedroll?" he rasped. His eyes glinted with an eldritch gold light.

"Everything. They still may track her scent." Brokk nodded at me, and I felt ashamed. "We need to get back to the mountain."

"Too late now," Leif said. "I scouted, and there's another force of draugr coming down the road. How did the Corpse King even know we'd raided the abbey?"

Brokk snorted. "The friar sent word, trying to save his wretched arse. Rolf and Thorbjorn chased him, but he locked himself in the scullery, and did a small spell to alert his master before they broke down the door. His workings didn't save him."

"He's dead?" I blurted.

"Aye," Brokk answered me. "Our fellow warriors did the deed."

My breath left in a rush. The nightmare who'd haunted my days was gone. But Sage and my friends had fallen into the hands of these strange warriors.

"We must be off. They are coming," Leif said. I let him pull me close. His hands slid around me, his touch already familiar. "We will hide until we are sure the Grey Men will not follow us."

"Grey Men?" I asked.

"They are corpses," Brokk said. "Men one step beyond the veil of death, animated by a mage's evil power."

"How is that possible?" I whispered.

"He is an ancient king with magic of old." Leif clutched me tighter, and I snuggled into his arms, my fingers gripping his smooth muscle. His scent surrounded me—a pleasing blend of woodsmoke and wild mint, with a hint of spice. "He has been defeated and locked in a near-death state, but over time found a way to fight. Like a spider drawing in his prey on the web, he sent his power out to create these Grey Men. They somehow convinced the friar to do his bidding. The Corpse King is coming back to life."

"He's found a new source of power and is coming after it," Brokk said.

"What source?" I asked.

Brokk glanced back, his eye glowing with a yellow light. "You."

LEIF

Stop scaring her, I sent to my warrior brother with a frown.

She needs to know the truth. Out loud, he said, "We need to find water. The Grey Men do not like it."

"There's a marsh nearby." We knew the terrain from our time staking out the abbey.

"It may be enough. But we'd better find a river, or better yet, a lake."

Willow's breath came in ragged gasps as we threaded through the woods. Brokk led, and I brought up the rear, touching her often to reassure her.

The thicket gave way to a ragged patch of reeds and muddy water. We went in, picking our way over the soggy terrain. The mud sucked at my boots, and I bit back a curse. If we were lucky, the swamp would be enough to deter the Corpse King's servants.

Brokk stopped then turned with a finger to his lips.

More draugr ahead. The wind blowing in our face holds their scent. They're hemming us in. Unless we cross the marsh, we need to hunker down and hope the Grey Men do not sense us. Brokk sounded brisk. We'd faced hopeless situations before. He stood aloof, away from me and the woman.

"We hide here until they pass and then continue on," I said out loud for Willow's benefit.

Brokk nodded. We all hunkered down for an uneasy wait. The sound of footsteps, a force of many men coming towards us, their stench on the wind. The beast leapt to the fore. I shut my eyes, willing it not to break free.

Leif?

I'm fine. I turned my head against the wind, and caught the scent of Willow's hair. Such a small and lovely little thing, trembling beside us with a fierce expression on her face. She'd been through so much tonight, and remained brave. I had to hang on, for her.

We can fight, Brokk offered. From his brittle tone, he did not think it a good idea. Even if we did clear a path for our escape, letting our beasts out tempted danger.

There's too many of them. I put a hand over my mouth and nose as a strong breeze blew up more of their stench. *The Corpse King sent a great force.*

He will do anything to possess his future brides.

A growl escaped me before I could stop it. Willow stiffened.

"Calm," Brokk murmured to both of us.

From where we crouched, the road shone in the moonlight. The force of draugr came up the path, macabre soldiers marching with jerky motions. A few had spears and swords, but most had pitchforks and staffs, ordinary items made into weapons. Rank upon rank trod towards us. How had the Corpse King conjured up such a force, so fast?

Odin's boots. They're not Grey Men. At least, their skin is not grey.

I craned my head over the marsh grasses. As Brokk said, the force did not look as thin and sallow as the Grey Men we'd faced before. These were men of all ages, with ruddy skin and blank expressions, wearing the garb of villagers.

The silent ranks passed not a few paces from where we hid, over a hundred of them. Brokk's intent face told me he was counting.

These draugr stink of blood, but not rotting flesh, I said, when more than half had passed.

They haven't been dead long. Brokk sounded more grim than usual.

A chill went through me.

The ranks had thinned when Willow sat up. "Joseph!" The name burst from her lips.

I pulled her down. "Quiet, lass."

But she struggled. "Wait. I know him from the village." I clapped my hand over her mouth.

"Stop," I hissed in her ear. She squawked in distress, loud enough to alert the enemy and arouse the beast.

Brokk put his face close to hers, his expression stern enough to make a man cower.

"You will be still. We are all in danger."

She shook her head as much as she could with my hand over her mouth but stopped struggling.

"The man you think you know? It is not him. Joseph is gone. The Corpse King's magic took his life and his mind and made him a tool of evil."

With a muffled cry, she sagged against me.

Too harsh? Brokk asked me.

I shook my head. Her eagerness to help her friend might be our death. If the enemy didn't march a mere few feet away, I'd put her over my knee and punish her. I shared this image with Brokk, and a corner of his mouth creased.

Perhaps punishing her would be his role, if it enticed him to accept our mate.

BROKK

I glared at Willow until she dropped her gaze. Wolves abide by strict rules of dominance, and we both knew she ceded to mine. But she must not only recognize my rule. She must obey. If I'd already accepted her as mate, she'd be in for a punishment. Once we found safety, I'd take a strap to her backside until it blazed red...

Careful, one part of me chastened. *You have played this game before.* I was one of the few Berserkers who remembered the folly of love. It ended in sorrow.

The Grey Men had almost all passed.

Perhaps I would take a strap to her, for her punishment and my pleasure. My beast couldn't wait to see her bared before us.

My cock perked up at the idea. I gritted my teeth.

"Little woman, you will obey," I told her in a harsh whisper. "You will do as we say and be quiet."

She shrank against Leif, and he put his arms around her. I turned from the pretty couple. Women always ran to Leif.

This is not the same, Leif said to me. *We will share her in all things.*

I shook my head. We couldn't have this conversation while our enemies passed a few feet away.

Not if we cannot fight our way away from the Grey Men.

For a moment, I wished Leif and I weren't bonded. If I had a choice, I should not share a woman, but the bond between us required we take the same mate.

You're glaring at her again, Leif told me. I blanked my features.

At this point, Willow is more frightened of us than the Grey Men. Talk to her. Tell her what's going on. Soothe her.

I did not have the gift for such sweet words. *You do it.*

She is to be your mate, as much as mine. Leif raised his chin.

The last of the Grey Men had marched on.

"Forgive me," I said to the frightened girl. "I am used to giving orders and having them obeyed. We are hiding because the Corpse King sent his servants to get you. They are dead men. Animated souls." The woman shivered. Leif put his arm around her.

"I don't understand. What does he want with me?" she asked.

"He seeks all spaewives for his own. He desires your power. He had you contained in the abbey and planned to take you one by one, to consume your power by draining your blood—"

"Enough," Leif interrupted. "Willow, listen to me. All you need know is you must stay with us and follow our lead." *We can explain the rest later,* he sent to me.

I drew in a breath, inhaling the woman's rich scent. At least the Grey Men hadn't sensed her. Under the miasma of mud and the draugr's stink, I smelled her heat, but it was faint. I wished we were far away, back at our home or somewhere safe where we could explore her body's wanton reaction to us.

"Let us go," I commanded. Leif nodded and rose. He would carry the woman so we could travel at Berserker speed.

"You will be quiet," I said to her. "We must travel past the village to escape."

"We must take care," Leif muttered. "There will be Grey Men everywhere."

"Let us hope they will not expect us."

I reached out to try to link to the pack, but the mental path felt blocked. *I cannot reach the Alphas,* I told Leif. The frown on his face told me he couldn't, either.

The Corpse King has great power. His magic must disrupt the bond.

We must take care. We cannot survive long on our own. The beast already felt agitated by the presence of our enemy and aroused by our new mate.

We will survive, Leif responded. *We have helped each other this long.*

I grunted. The magic linking us saved our lives, even if I often resented it. It wasn't like either of us had a choice.

I turned my thoughts to strategy. *The rest of our brothers must be scattered. I fear our way home is blocked. If I were the Corpse King, I'd set an ambush on the route to the mountain and recover as many women as possible.*

We cannot return, then. We must keep Willow safe.

I agreed. Leif lifted the woman in his arms, and she let out a soft yelp.

"Do we have to gag you?" I asked her.

She shook her head.

"Quickly, then." I led the way up the road, dipping into the forest when we neared the abbey. Whatever cold mist had passed Leif's hiding place seemed to have wilted the grass and plants in a wide circle. Even the trees looked brittle and aged, as if coated with a layer of frost.

Odin's blood. Our detour would take us right through the village. Axe raised at the ready, I crept back to the road, expecting to see ranks of Grey Men waiting in the moonlight, a living barricade.

Well, not living, but a formidable barrier, nonetheless.

The wind picked up, and I sniffed it. A faint smell of blood, but no draugr.

"Stop," I told Leif and Willow. "Let me go on alone." *Keep her safe.*

Leif nodded, and I went forward. The scent of blood hung thick over each home, and quiet reigned throughout the village, from the rudest hut to the empty center square.

Tingles ran up and down my spine as the curse gathered energy for the Change. I'd been on battlefields before and felt the same oppressive silence. But something told me we hadn't stumbled on the aftermath of a fight, but a slaughter.

My boot splashed into a great puddle of mud, and the scent of rust filled my nose. I stopped.

Stooping, I touched the pool in front of one dark house. My finger came away wet, but not with water.

Blood.

I went to the door. At my heavy tread, it creaked open.

With a wary hand, I pushed farther. Smoke filled the house, remnants of a dying fire. It took a moment for my eyes to adjust, but once they did, I saw what I expected.

I closed the door and said a prayer for the dead within before striding from house to house, checking for signs of life.

Each house lay in darkness but for a few with dwindling fires. I knew now how so many draugr had appeared, almost out of nowhere. The cold scent still lingered—the Corpse King's magic had swept through and claimed the minds of the able-bodied men. The Grey Men we'd seen were all villagers, changed. Before they left for the Corpse King's service, they had killed everyone they'd leave behind.

"Odin's eyes," I muttered as I passed house after house littered with the dead. A few lay in doorways, some in the streets. Old ones, women, and children.

No one had survived.

Go around the village, I sent to Leif. *Do not allow Willow to see this.*

I checked the last house, but the slaughter was complete. Picking up a blanket, I covered the remains of a dead mother and child. "Go in peace," I told them. If I had time, I would bury the bodies and call a witch to purify the area with salt and fire. But we had to keep moving before the Corpse King's spells swept through again. I whispered a quick prayer, knowing it would not be enough to keep the dead spirits from lingering here, crying for justice.

I stepped out of the hut, eager to breathe air clear of blood and tainted magic.

Brokk, where are you? The scent of blood...the beast...I can't...

Hold on, Leif!

I heard a slight cry and whirled in time to catch Willow in my arms. Too late; she saw the still and bloody arm of the woman, most likely severed when she flung it out to protect her child from the killing blow.

"No," Willow sobbed, reaching for the dead woman's hand.

"Come," I grunted, lifting her. Her fingers clawed at my arms as I strode away. *Leif, I've got her.*

She would not stop struggling. Leif sounded tired and sad.

I bit back my retort. The scent of slaughter brought out the beast. Leif struggled to maintain control.

I will carry her. Go ahead and scout for us. The Corpse King may have left a few Grey Men here to stand guard.

I turned my attention to the woman fighting to break out of my hold.

"Stop, I know her. Margaret. Joseph's wife. We must bury her."

"There's too many. The whole village has been slaughtered," I bit out, and cursed myself for telling her as sorrow contorted her face.

"No," she moaned.

I forced her head down against my shoulder. "Close your eyes," I barked. She sobbed against me as we passed the silent houses, the bodies in the blood-soaked streets.

Leif, quickly. We must get out of here.

You...go...

"Odin's blood," I cursed. *Hang on.* I dodged between homes, heading for the forest. *We have our woman now. You must keep control.*

In the shadows, Leif growled.

I leapt back. "Leif, it's me."

Brokk!

I ducked, and a spear flew over my head. The Grey Men had found us.

Leif charged out of the woods. I feinted and dodged again, but he ran past me to attack the advancing draugr.

Get her out. Go! A howl rang out, loud and haunting. Enough to send an ordinary man scrambling. The hunting cry of a Berserker.

I fled into the forest, crashing through the brush, Willow in my arms. She clung to me.

"Odin's breath," I muttered as I splashed into a swift-running stream. I followed it to its end and set Willow down, freeing a hand in case the Grey Men followed. Leif would make short work of the small group of men left to guard the village. I only hoped I could call him back when he'd finished killing. I should not leave him.

Willow leaned against me, her features fixed in silent horror. She did not cry out again.

I tucked her in tighter. When I touched Leif's mind, I found red rage and madness, the tainted power of the Berserker curse.

Come back to us, I called, and sent him an impression of what I felt—the soft, lovely, and trembling body of a woman against mine. *Our mate is waiting.*

No answer. He battled both the Grey Men, and the beast, spitting out a disgusting mouthful of draugr flesh.

Willow sagged in my arms.

"They all...they're all dead," she mumbled.

She was weeping, and I didn't know what to say.

"Do not grieve for them." I gripped her, my voice savage. "They lived near enough to the abbey to know the friar mistreated you, and they did nothing."

Her mouth opened and shut. Nothing came out.

"Be grateful the end was swift. It will not be the same for us, if the Corpse King catches up."

She stared at me.

Come quickly, I called to Leif. *I cannot do this alone.*

"Odin's staff," I said out loud. Brushing her hair back with a clumsy hand, I smeared her skin with blood. Cursing louder, I bent and washed my hand in the stream and wiped the stain away.

Willow seemed frozen.

"You're all right," I told her. "We got out alive."

"It was you," she said in a horrified whisper. "You did it."

"Willow, no."

"You brought them on. We were fine until you arrived."

She fought me. I let her, standing motionless while her tiny fists beat my armored chest.

I caught her wrists before she did damage to herself.

"Stop." I growled. "You are not thinking clearly. We came to rescue you."

"Liar. They're all dead. You killed them—"

"The Corpse King killed them. He came for you. Do you understand? It is your magic, your flesh he desires above all. This—" I plunged my hand between her legs, cupping her sex. "This is what calls to him. Your scent when you are in heat."

At my crude touch, she stilled, but it sickened me to manhandle her. I took my hand away.

"We saved you, Willow. You and your sisters at the abbey would be dead, or enslaved, if we had not come. We are trying to help you."

She shook her head, mouth working with silent protest.

I shook her. If she panicked again and screamed, she might have the whole enemy force running to us. I had to make her see.

Brokk. Enough. Give her to me. Leif stepped from the shadows. His eyes shone with the beast's magic, but he'd Changed back into the form of the man.

Leif? Are you sure?

He snarled and Willow cried out. "What is that?"

"It's Leif," I said, smoothing my hands down her thin arms. "He feels distress because you are in pain."

"Leif?" she quavered, and my warrior brother came forward, his features human and handsome once more.

I relinquished my bundle and stepped back. To my

surprise, Willow ran from me, threw her arms around Leif's shoulders, and hugged him close.

After a pause, his arms closed around her. They still bore tufts of fur.

Leif...

I know. He adjusted his hold, pressing her face into his neck as she cried. Leif let out grunting, soothing sounds, more animal than man, but when I touched his mind, I found quiet. His rage had retreated.

She calms the beast, I said, shocked.

Leif gave a sharp nod. *At a great price. The Corpse King will sacrifice anything and anyone to retrieve his intended brides.* The woman's sniffling had subsided, but Leif kept his hand on her head. "You're safe now," he said out loud, and to me *—Let us go before more Grey Men come.*

Following my warrior brother, I stepped from the stream. We melted into the woods.

LEIF

I do not like how pale our little captive looks.

We'd spent the night crossing hard terrain, heading north and east, away from the pack and home. I carried Willow, cradling her to my chest when she fell into a doze. Within me, the beast also slept, content. Willow had stilled it with her scent and trusting touch.

She leaned against my shoulder as Brokk and I ran together under the silent moon.

She's not afraid of us. She sleeps, Brokk observed.

She is exhausted. And once we find safety, there is much to tell her. Other than her pallor, she seemed healthy, if a little thin. Her arms and legs bore muscles made sturdy from work.

Let's get a good meal into her, Brokk agreed. *I know a place to take shelter. It's quiet and out-of-the-way. We will stay there until we can reach the Alphas.*

They will expect us back at the mountain.

They will know something is wrong. The Corpse King's forces have us scattered. They did a good job of isolating us, the better to pick us off and take the mage's brides back, one by one.

They will not take her, I growled and clutched my fragrant-smelling bundle close.

They will not take her, Brokk echoed. In this, my warrior brother and I shared one mind. He'd always been more wary and slower to trust, but he had seen how the beast responded to her presence.

My little miracle. She had a few freckles on her face. I wanted to kiss each one. There would be time for that, once we had her safe. I just had to convince Brokk to accept her.

When we came to a river, I paused on the bank. *Here. You are taller. Why don't you carry her over?*

Brokk snorted. He stood taller by a hairsbreadth; we joked of it often.

But you are stronger and uglier. More suited to being a beast of burden.

Suit yourself. I waded in, holding the woman high. *I will be first in everything. First to find her. First to carry her. First to fuck her.*

Brokk grimaced at me, showing his fangs.

We must seduce her first, he said, and I sobered.

Do you think she suffered ill-use, like the woman Rolf and Thorbjorn wish to claim?

Even if she escaped the friar's attentions, she still suffered under their threat, Brokk pointed out and I agreed.

He's dead now?

Good and dead. Thorbjorn told me the moment it happened. He struck the friar down before the Grey Men swarmed the place.

We crossed the river and continued to make haste. No sense lingering, even if the Grey Men couldn't follow. The Corpse King had other weapons.

We must charm her, I said, after a few minutes' silence. *Put her at ease.*

You're better at wooing women, Brokk said. Did he realize his scowl held a measure of pain?

If I can control the beast. I tried to joke, but no Berserker would laugh at such a serious subject. We'd all seen comrades die when the beasts ate their minds and filled them with endless rage. If a wolf lost control, the pack must put him down.

In my arms, Willow let out a little sigh. The weather had turned cold, too cold for late summer.

I shifted her in my arms. *Let's get out of this wind.*

We are close to shelter. Brokk led the way, winding uphill until we came to a grassy knoll, high above the trees. The forest had been cleared to make way for a castle fort, now abandoned and in ruins.

The king of this land misjudged his power. His enemy overtook him before he finished building his fortress, and the mercenaries knocked most of it down. Brokk's mouth curved in a grim smile.

"When did this happen?" I said aloud, keeping my voice low so as not to wake her. Brokk and I could link mind to mind, able to share thoughts, images and impressions, but he liked his privacy. We tended to use the bond only in the direst need. Except for today, when we used it for Willow's comfort.

"A few decades ago. I went with Knut, Rolf, and Thorbjorn. The opposing king hired us." He shrugged. "A day's entertainment to take the fort and slaughter every man inside. Well worth the purse of gold." We climbed the hill and stepped out onto the ledge overlooking a vast, still lake. The wind ruffled the blue-black water. "We spent some time standing here, throwing stones into the lake." Brokk pointed.

"Where was I?" I asked, even though I could guess.

Brokk unslung the pack and went to the tallest wall still standing. He shook out a bedroll and wolf skin, making a soft nest for the woman. "You had sought solitude...to control your beast."

I laid our little captive down on the makeshift bed. She let out a soft sigh, burrowing into the fur, and slept on. The events of the night—her fighting, terror, and tears—left her worn out. Her small fingers gripped the fur.

I nudged Brokk. "Perhaps she would be more comfortable with the wolf."

Brokk pressed his lips together. "She needs to learn to trust us as mates."

My head snapped up. "You accept her, then?"

Brokk grunted. I stood guard over the woman while he made camp and built up a fire. He kept his distance and did not glance our way, but once the blaze took hold, he stripped off his clothes, folded them in the pack, and Changed. A giant black wolf with brown markings trotted over to settle near the sleeping woman. His bulk and the wall shielded her from the wind.

Chuckling, I rose to tend the fire.

BROKK

Our little woman slept with her soft cheek cradled in her hands. I napped nearby as a wolf naps, in fits and starts, rising often to turn and resettle in my bed. Leif left to hunt, and I kept my eyes open, wary lest she come awake and think her fine redheaded suitor had abandoned her to a feral wolf.

Dawn came creeping over the hills, and the birds rejoiced. Hundreds of white-wings gathered by the lakeshore, a long jump and short run away from the ruined fort. If I were not guarding my new mate, I'd go and frighten them, barking at their beating wings, trying to catch one for my breakfast. A fine pastime for a morning.

Beside me, the little female slept on, face twisted in a worried expression. I laid my head on my paws and sighed.

Leif returned with a pair of rabbits, already skinned. He had them cooking by the time the woman stirred. With a glance at me, he came to take my place while I went behind the low wall. I couldn't keep from peeking over it to watch her chest rise and fall in sleep.

When Willow cried out and woke with a start, Leif crouched close to comfort her.

"It's all right." He held his hands out. "Hush, lass. You're safe now."

She licked her lips. "Where am I?"

"A temporary camp. We'll stay a few nights, until we're sure it's safe. Then it's back to our home, where you'll be reunited with your friends. Come," he beckoned. "Come sit by the fire. There's nothing here for you to fear."

Just as he'd convinced her to rise and follow him, a bird cried out. She jerked around, and her gaze fell on me.

"Calm, Willow," Leif crooned, but his soothing murmur didn't stop her from scrabbling backwards until her back hit the broken wall. She pressed against the grey-green stones, trembling.

"There's a wolf," she whispered.

"I know. He's a friend. Here." He nodded to me, and I poked my head around the edge of the stones.

Mate, the wolf hummed when it caught her scent. I almost gave her a wide, toothy grin before I remembered myself. The sloping wall didn't quite hide my large form, even crouching. When I stood tall, I'd be able to lick her chin without much strain.

"Where did it come from?"

Leif paused, debating how much to tell her. "He's been with us all along. Don't worry. He's well tamed."

He winked at me, and I glared at him. Grinning, the warrior went back to making our meal. Willow stayed crouched against the wall, though she picked up the wolf pelt and put it around her shoulders. I crept from the wall, taking my place at the warrior's side.

You're cooking them too much, I told him, as the rabbit's flesh turned an unappetizing brown.

"Weren't you going to go chase birds on the beach?" Leif asked me out loud. The wolf had let the bond drift open between us. The wolf part of us desired connection over privacy.

Besides, I found it harder to keep the bond closed when I felt happy or content—or maybe I preferred it open, as if sharing with my warrior brother made my joy complete.

"Chase birds?" Willow asked.

"Just talking to wolfie here." He gestured and I let out a low growl.

Wolfie?

Better than ugly. Leif continued, "He wanted to go down to the lake earlier. Perhaps you could go fetch water with him."

"You talk to him?" Willow's eyes widened until they seemed to take up half her face, but she'd stepped away from the wall. Her black hair blew in the wind. I wanted to go curl up at her feet.

"Of course. He and I have long been companions, right, wolfie?"

I let out a high-pitched bark, as close to a dog's as I could make it.

Willow took another step closer, and glanced around the keep. "Is Brokk here?"

"He'll be back, soon enough," Leif smirked.

This is ridiculous, Leif. Just tell her it's me.

Not until you've earned her trust as a great furry beast. Did I ever tell you you're much nicer as a wolf?

I raised a lip, showing my teeth in a silent half snarl.

Certainly better looking. Smirking, Leif pulled my share of the meat from the flame—still half-raw—and tossed it to me. I caught it in my mouth and ambled away to take my meal overlooking the lake and the birds. Willow didn't need to see me tear apart flesh and bone.

I ducked my head to keep from smelling the roasted rabbit. The wolf preferred raw, but the scent seemed to draw Willow away from the wall. My ears pricked up as she ventured near the fire, sitting on a stone near Leif. He waited until she'd settled before slicing off bits of the meat.

"Here." He sat, too. "Taste this."

He held it up, tsking when she tried to take it with her fingers. She blushed as he bade her open her mouth and eat from his hand like a little bird, but her stomach growled and overruled her embarrassment. A tender smile played over Leif's lips as he fed her.

See, Brokk? She will become used to us. And then... Then we would seduce her, eventually stripping away all her defenses and claiming her. A mating bond would form between the three of us, two monsters in man-form and the lithe and lovely woman with the power to break our curse. It seemed almost too easy.

Too easy? We've waited over a century for her, battling the beast.

I did not respond.

"How did you become friends with a wolf?" Willow asked.

"He saved my life, I saved his." Leif kept up the ruse. He liked this game. Then again, telling lies in the middle of truth was a particular gift of my silver-tongued friend.

Leif frowned when he caught the echo of my thought.

It will not be like before, Brokk. You must believe me.

I rose and carried my meat bones around the wall so I could crunch them with animal savagery.

Willow watched me go.

∼

By midafternoon, I itched to run in the forest, but the wolf wanted to remain close to his mate. She sat nearby, and, when I stayed very still, she relaxed. Her curiosity outweighed her fear.

"You can touch him," Leif invited. "He's harmless. See." He rose and came to my side. "He will let me pet him."

If I bite off your hand, it will not grow back.

You won't bite me. Leif ran his hand down my back. *Not while she's watching.*

I endured the petting. My warrior brother kept it blessedly brief.

"Now your turn, Willow," Leif coaxed her over.

I held my breath as she approached. I saw the moment she decided to be brave. She paused as if weighing her fears then went ahead anyway, with the same determination Leif had noticed when we first met her. No hesitation.

She stroked my back with small white fingers. Relaxed under her touch, I felt a quiver deep within, my beast stirring as it recognized my greatest longing would soon be satisfied. I laid my head on my paws, eyes closing in pleasure as she played with my ears.

"See?" Leif said. "He likes it."

Willow kept petting me. She relaxed, but her hands felt cold. When I Changed back into a man, the magic might leave me with a pelt about my shoulders. I would give her each fur and shift as often as I could until I could build her a bed piled with wolf skins. My mate would sleep in comfort she'd never known before.

The wolf let out a satisfied growl, muted so as not to scare our timid prey. It liked the idea of Willow surrounded by my scent.

By midday, she sat right next to me and didn't smell nervous at all.

Leif fed her, and she once went behind a wall to relieve herself, but when she returned, she curled up again by my side. She seemed to draw comfort from me, a wonder I scarce believed.

I told you. Leif sounded smug.

"Are my friends all right?" she asked, twisting her fingers together. With a small whine, I nudged her, and she stroked my nose instead.

"They all are protected," Leif answered, with a glance at me. We hadn't been able to reach the pack via the bond. Too many leagues and too much dark magic disrupting even the Alphas' power. "Not all of them are out of danger. We know the Grey Men attacked."

"What are the Grey Men?" she asked.

"Servants of the Corpse King, an evil mage who wishes the world to be under his rule. He draws power by wedding and bedding your kind."

"My kind?"

"Aye. You have magic in your blood. You're a special race of women, with power that allows you to..." he hesitated, but Willow's eyes were focused on the lake beyond Leif.

"Magic," she breathed. "How can that be?"

"We think the magic remains latent until you are wed." Leif, ever the charmer, phrased things in a way she might understand.

My wolf snorted. Wolves did not wed, they mated, and for life. A Berserker bond ran deeper than a human vow. Once Willow linked to us, mind to mind, we would be as one.

The brother bond Leif and I used to share power allowed us to share a woman as well. If we had not bonded, sharing a woman would be impossible. We would fight to the death, and succumb to the beast, our salvation just out of reach.

"I don't believe in magic." Willow wrapped her arms around her small body.

"What of your gods? You lived in a holy place, among the devout. Have you never seen their power?"

"No." She drew her legs up to her chest, shrinking in on herself. "I pray and pray, but no one answers," she mumbled, almost to herself.

"What about witches and seers?"

"The friar speaks out against them."

"Some men hate what they do not understand. Or what they cannot control," Leif said, and for once I felt grateful for his silver tongue. "There is evil, but there is also good."

The woman raised her head. I butted her hand until she petted me again.

"The magic you possess is a subtle thing. It manifests in an affinity for herbs and healing. Surely you have that gift."

"If there is magic like that in the world, I do not have any," she said. "I have suffered a sickness all my life."

"What is the nature of the sickness?" Leif asked.

After glancing at the horizon, where the moon would soon rise, she shook her head.

"What if I could prove to you there is magic?" Leif said.

Careful. I stiffened. *This is not a game.*

She is strong. Let us give her the truth. We owe it to her.

Let it be on your head, then. My words tasted bitter. His folly would not rest on his head, but on mine. Always on mine.

Willow sat still and trusting as I padded to the center of

empty keep. The sun shone high above us. I could see every freckle, every dark eyelash on Willow's cheek as she blinked.

I hope this is the right choice.

Leif stayed silent. He and I tread on new hunting ground. We'd never lured a mate before, but we always got our prey.

I raised my wolf head and Changed. The magic crept from tailbone to nape and back again. Sometimes it hurt, but this time it didn't. A soft wind blew through the keep as I stretched and rose out of the wolf form.

By the time I stood as a man, naked but for the loincloth at my hips and pelt around my shoulders, the woman had crawled back against the wall and huddled there. She trembled, biting her lip, blinking back tears.

"It's all right," I rasped, my voice hoarse as my throat struggled to remember how to form human words.

Her distress called to the darker part of me. Not wolf, not man, but the deep hunger of the beast. It wanted to destroy her enemies then lay her down and claim her, make her know she would always be ours.

"Brokk," Leif snapped, and I stopped moving towards the fragile female. In the end, he went to her and comforted her, while I slipped away. I would Change back into a wolf and go on the hunt. I'd rather chase down prey than to stare into a frightened woman's eyes.

LEIF

"Willow, be calm. All is well. There is magic in us, but it will not harm you." At least, it would not if we mated soon enough to keep the beast quiet.

She shook her head and stayed tucked against the wall, her arms around her legs. I hated the raw sorrow on her face. She'd begun to give us her trust, and I had broken it.

I let her be for the rest of the afternoon. She stayed stiff and silent. When she shivered, she would not even let me come close to tuck a fur around her. I dropped the wolf pelt nearby, but once I turned my back, she picked it up and flung it away. I bit back a grin when she glared. I much preferred her anger to her sadness. When she finished sulking, I would find a new way to woo her.

A few times I tried to reach out to the pack, but the link remained faint. We'd strayed out of distance of even the Alphas' strong call. Or the Corpse King had found a way to disrupt our bond as we'd believed he might.

The mere thought of our powerful enemy brought my

beast to the fore. I hid my hands as my nails lengthened. Gritting my teeth, I resisted the Change.

Brokk. You must return. We both must bond with her soon. I tried to draw strength from my warrior brother, as I had done many times before. Under the pretense of relieving myself, I stepped behind the wall and braced against the grey-green stones, willing my body to remain a man's. We'd already frightened Willow once today. I prayed she'd never meet the monster we could become, the Berserker beast.

Brokk. Brother. Please.

He kept blocking me. Sunset approached, and I didn't trust my own control.

You cannot leave me alone with her, Brokk. It is not safe. Damn him for making me beg. I'd always been the weaker one. He took pleasure in reminding me.

"Leif?" Willow called.

"One moment," I barked, my voice thick as my throat. My head throbbed with the ache of resisting the Change, but at last I regained control and came out from behind the wall.

She had risen but hadn't stepped from her spot. "May I have some water?"

I forced a smile. "Of course, lass. We will go down to the lake."

She came to my side. I'd removed the tether and my arm ring from around her throat the night before, and as much as I admired her lovely neck, I missed the sight of my silver collaring it.

"Give me your word you will not try to run. These woods are strange to us. I do not know what lurks here."

"I will not run."

"If you do, I will let Brokk punish you."

Her scent flared, and the musk of her arousal made my

cock respond. For a moment, my vision swam, but the beast did not seize control. It watched, waiting in the shadows, curious about the small, fragile being frowning up at me.

"You like the idea of punishment?"

"What? No." She took a step back.

I growled, low in my throat. "Do not run from me, Willow. I will chase and catch you without much effort." Her scent blazed hotter, the longing of a spaewife, eager for my claim. "I'm warning you, lass. I am more predator than man. But if you do as I say, you will be safe."

She gnawed her lips, her thoughts warring across her face. Part of her wanted to run; part of her did not.

"We will go to the lake," I told her. "You will stay by my side, and obey. Or do you wish to risk running into the arms of the Grey Men?" The Corpse King's servants should not come close to this place, but we must take care.

Shuddering, she shook her head. "I give you my word. I will not run."

"Then, come." At first, she ignored my outstretched hand, so I took her wrist instead.

Her pulse jumped under my touch. I led her, my cock growing harder with each step. The beast needed to claim, to protect, to dominate. Willow invited all three. I couldn't imagine anyone more perfect.

I took her to a little stream that fed the lake, so she could drink the sweet, clear water. She crouched before me, filling her cupped hands. She drank until her pale cheeks flushed pink under her wild black hair. I quenched my thirst, staying alert to our surroundings. My nose told me we remained safe, but the Corpse King had many weapons. If he found us, he might weave a spell and catch us unaware.

A fox peered at us from the briar. I showed my teeth, and let the predator into my eyes. The creature fled.

Willow watched me as I studied the black lake through the trees. My wolf preened, enjoying her attention.

I winked at her, and a little furrow appeared between her eyes. Mine must be golden with the beast's magic.

"Are you also..." She paused, licking her lips.

"A wolf?" I finished for her. "Yes, I am. It is a long story, but I will keep it brief. Brokk and I are warriors of old. We fought for a king in the North Lands. He sent a band of his greatest warriors to a witch, thinking her spells would make us mighty." I fell silent for a moment. I didn't wish to explain the pride, the fierce elation at being chosen to become the best of the best. Or the horror when we woke and felt the beast stir within us, our hands still bloody from the first slaughter of innocents, our lives forever cursed.

"Did her spells work?"

"They made us very powerful, but power always carries a price."

I took her wrist again and we walked around the castle.

"You are Norseman?"

"Yes." I found a tree with hard, green apples and tossed one to her. "We came to this island to claim it for Harald Fair Hair, but remained."

Her brow wrinkled. "That king ruled many years ago."

"Over a hundred. Our lifespans have been lengthened. An effect of dealing with magic."

She paled again.

"You've heard of Harald Fair Hair. You know your history?"

She gave a stiff nod. "A few traveling monks visited the abbey. They were kind to the orphans and taught my friend and I a few things."

"Tell me about your friends."

"My friends?"

I nodded.

"We all came at different times and ages. My closest friends are Sage, Laurel, and Ivy. Also Angelica, Sorrel, and Rosalind, but they are younger."

I bit into my apple. "All orphans?"

"Some came when their parents died. Others came from families with too many children to feed. Their parents gave them up—those are the ones who aren't named for plants. Sage and I came as babes." She toyed with her apple, adding in a low voice, "I never knew my mother."

I tossed my apple core away. Brokk and I had left our family behind so long ago we didn't remember them. I could not comfort her, but soon there would be no need. Brokk and I would be her family.

"All of you are spaewives."

The furrow between her brows returned. "Everyone living at the abbey?"

"Perhaps not all of the holy women, but certainly all of the orphans. The friar only took in female orphans, correct?"

She nodded.

"I would stake my life on it. You all have a natural magic, an affinity with the earth. Do any of you make herbs or tinctures? Medicines your priest frowned upon because they always seem to work?"

"Yes," she replied. "We all do, but that is part of our duties. We're not witches."

"Spaewives aren't quite witches. Your magic comes from deep inside."

Willow wrung her hands, staring at the ground.

"We will not know what special abilities you have. But you have time to learn. There is one more sign, the mark of a spaewife ready to come into her full power."

"What's that?"

"The mating heat," I drawled, and savored her expression.

Pink flooded her cheeks. I should not enjoy taunting her, but she responded so prettily.

"I do not know anything about that." She whirled and began the climb back to the keep.

When I caught her arm, she resisted. "Careful, little captive." I tapped my nose. "Wolves can smell a lie." I leaned in closer. "Do you know what else we can smell?"

Her deep blush was quite fetching. I almost sent the image to Brokk before I remembered he still blocked me.

"The heat allows you to bind forever to a magical creature. That's why the Corpse King seeks you so fervently. He wants you to be his bride."

She laughed, a shaky sound.

"What is it, Willow?"

"Nothing." She shook her head. "A day ago, I had barely spoken to a man. Now you tell me a mage wants to marry me. It is unbelievable."

"Why?" I asked, and when she didn't answer, I said, "The mage is not the only one who seeks you for this purpose."

Her head snapped up. "You mean—"

"Aye, Willow. You are the perfect Berserker bride."

WILLOW

"**B**erserker?" I squeaked. "Is that what you are?"

"Yes." Leif's grin was white and pointy.

I tugged my hand away from him. "So I am to be your bride."

He inclined his head, still smug. I wanted to slap his face.

"And we live where? Here?" I cast a hand towards the ruins. The place seemed fitting enough. Isolated, wild. "Or in a forest den?"

Leif's face tightened. "No. We're taking you to the mountain, our home. We will live near the rest of the pack, in a lodge we'll build for you." His fingers caught a strand of my hair and tucked it behind my ear. His voice softened a touch. "You belong to us, Willow, and above all, we care for our mate."

I took a deep breath. "All right." How could I argue? Each passing moment they told me something more outrageous than the last.

I'd spent the day thinking of how I could escape. The best plan I'd come up with was to bide my time and befriend them until they dropped their guard. But the full moon rose tonight. What would I do then?

Leif prowled behind me as I climbed up the hill to the keep. The hair on the back of my neck raised as if a silent predator stalked me. Which, I supposed, one did.

I sat on the broken wall while the warrior built up the fire. I shouldn't indulge myself watching him, but I did anyway. His stunning face drew my eye. His hands made quick work of the chores, strong and sure. I couldn't help imagining them stroking my breasts. And his every glance my way sparked fire, as quickly as the flames caught the brush he'd stacked in the center of the keep.

The moon rose slowly, along with my dread. Soon, my heat would come upon me, and I would have a new captor to resist—my own lust.

My skin prickled. Leif stood behind me, his scent wafting my way. "What are you thinking about, Willow?" His hair brushed my shoulder, his breath warming my ear.

"Nothing." I turned my back on the setting sun. Leif stood close enough we almost touched. I put my hands behind my back so I would not yield to temptation.

He cocked his head. "You have not fought me yet."

"Should I?"

"I expected you to refuse to become our mate. If you have doubts, I'll do my best to convince you." He smirked, his canines on display.

"I thought the friar planned to sell us to any man who offered a bride price great enough to tempt him to give up his source of free labor at the looms or in the apothecary." I shrugged and worded my words so I did not lie but still made Leif think I wasn't planning on running away. "Everything we were taught prepared us to accept our fate. This is no different." Except my heart leaped whenever I came near him or Brokk. Energy buzzed through me as if my skin anticipated their touch. I crossed my arms over my chest. "Even the friar sometimes took what he wanted from us. He never touched me, but he told us we must submit to a man's desires."

Leif glared at me. "We are nothing like the friar. We will not force you, or touch you until you are ready. Your body will burn until you cry out and ask for our hands upon you."

With a half gasp, half sob, I pulled away. How had he known my thoughts?

Leif continued in a softer voice, "You will not submit to our desires but your own."

"It's wrong," I said. "You have the wrong woman. You should take me back." Maybe I could convince them to let me go. I could find a way to survive, beg for work. I'd find a new village and become a servant to earn my keep. "You do not want me."

Fingers curled around my arm, tugging me to face him once more. I couldn't fight, but I refused to meet his gaze.

"Willow," he murmured. "You do not know how much we want you. No matter. It is our delight to teach you. We've been searching for one such as you from the moment the witch cursed us."

"What?"

"A part of us is tainted. We call it the beast, and it struggles to break free. When it does, it will rage upon this island. Kill every living thing and turn it into a wasteland, much like the Corpse King wishes to do. You are the only one who stands in its way. The only one who can tame our beast."

"Me? How can I? I do not even know my own power."

"You do not but you will learn," he said. "It will be our honor to teach you."

"What about my sister orphans? What will the pack...?"

Leif watched me patiently.

"No." I backed away.

"It's all right, Willow. They are safe. They will be mated to my friends, who will treat them with care."

"You must let them go." My argument would not sway him, but I had to try. Sage would not want to be a bride. She would not even want a man to touch her. I didn't, either, but my body had a will of its own.

"They will not be harmed," Leif soothed.

"You don't understand. It is better for us to be secluded, away from the presence of men."

"You do not like men?" Leif cocked his head to the side. "Then why is the air filled with your scent?"

The shadows hid my blush. "Please don't speak of that," I whispered.

"Are you afraid, little one?" Leif frowned.

"She's not afraid of us," a deep voice rang out from beyond the wall. "She's afraid of herself."

BROKK

I strode around the broken stones, bowed under the weight of the huge buck I'd slaughtered. The last of the dying sun's rays followed me as I traipsed to the fire and slung my kill down.

"Any trouble on the hunt?" Leif asked.

I grunted negative. I'd spent the afternoon gutting and preparing the carcass, hanging it from a high branch to drain out while my wolf enjoyed the offal. The buck would feed us for a while. The next time I wanted to leave, I'd have to come up with a new excuse.

"We shall have a feast," Leif announced, eyes shining.

"I'll cut branches to make a spit," he continued, drawing his axe and hopping over the wall nearest the lake. An ordinary man wouldn't survive the drop, but, a moment later, his red head bobbed towards the forest.

Coward. I called after him.

It's your turn to woo her. He'd already forgiven me for leaving him alone with the woman for so long.

Willow rushed halfway to the wall Leif had jumped over, but stopped short of passing me. "Is he all right?"

"Yes. Do not trouble yourself about him. Not much can kill a Berserker." I'd caught some of their conversation via the bond. Leif kept his mind open to me, as if the rat knew I could not resist spying.

I went about readying the buck for the fire. Willow hung back. For a moment, I thought she might speak about the morning's events, but she said nothing.

You can talk to her, too, you know. Leif sent.

"Odin's beard, will you never be quiet?"

"What?" Willow asked.

"Nothing." Better I stay silent, lest I frighten our captive and send her running to cry in Leif's arms again. The memory made my motions savage. I tore the buck's legs off before I realized an ordinary man would never be able to do such a thing.

Willow's face paled under her few freckles, but she hadn't yet fled.

"Sorry," I muttered and moved to block her view of my work.

She paced closer. Back and forth, back and forth, and the dying bonfire crackled to life. Once Willow had finished feeding it, she dusted off her hands, standing closer to me than I expected.

I hated how excited she made me feel.

"You left for a long time," she said.

I grunted.

"This is a large buck," she added after a few minutes. "Are we to stay here long?"

"Long enough. We can kill the Grey Men, but there are many of them, and we will not risk your safety. Leif told you the truth. We have searched many years to find women who could break our curse. We will not risk you. This is the first time we found so many Grey Men in one place."

"The Corpse King." Leif returned, carrying a sapling stripped clean. "He likes to collect spaewives."

"Collect us?"

"Yes." I fixed her with a stern look. "He hunts you still, so it is important you stay close and heed every word we say."

She swallowed and hovered near as we spitted the buck.

"Why would he want us?"

"He feeds his magic with the blood of spaewives," I said.

Brokk, Leif cautioned. "You have magic, Willow. You are of a special race."

"You don't believe us?" I asked.

Willow shook her head. "You are the first to tell me of this."

"It's true, Willow," Leif said. "You came to the abbey as a babe—"

"Because my mother gave me up—"

"She did not give you up," I snapped. "I wager the Grey Men sensed her magical blood, took her, and left you in the abbey to grow up."

I knew I'd said the wrong thing when Willow turned whiter.

"My mother," she whispered.

I remembered too late what she had seen in the village. Her face screwed up, and she turned away.

Why did you say such a thing? Leif asked, rushing to her side.

I scowled.

"Come here, lass. It's all right. You're all right."

"No." She wiped her eyes. "You're lying to me. I won't listen to you." She ran from the keep.

"Go to her." Leif clenched his fists at his side, dark fur rippling down his arms. His eyes glowed. His beast lurked too close for him to chase her.

Still, I balked. "Me? What can I do?"

"Use your words. Calm her."

I shook my head. I did not know how to be sweet and caring. I was a warrior. I knew nothing of wooing a woman. But I'd do anything to stop her weeping.

Willow sat on a low wall on the edge of the keep, facing the lake. She still wore the pelt about her shoulders, clutching it close. The gesture gave me hope.

I sat down on the wall, some distance from her.

"I apologize. I often say or do the wrong thing. They call me Stone Face," I admitted. "I am like a rock in battle, but I have a clumsy tongue."

She smiled a little but without joy.

"It's all so much." She wiped her eyes.

I heaved a sigh.

Go to her, Leif said. *Put your arm around her.*

Get out of my head, I told him, but without malice.

"Come to me," I ordered, and held out a hand to her. She shied at first. I watched her gnaw her lip then decide. Picking up her skirts, she did as I bid.

I did not wait for her to protest. I folded her into my arms, holding her head to my chest. She quivered and stilled. With a little sigh, Willow relaxed her soft body against me. I waited a blissful minute, inhaling the sweet scent of her hair. Our hearts thumped as one.

"I am not a kind man," I told her. "My words are a dull knife. I am not clever like Leif. But I will tell you this, Willow." Shifting, I gathered her hair back so my hand could cradle her throat. "If I had known the day the Grey Men came to take you from your mother, I would've watched over you then. From this day forward, your enemies are my enemies, and nothing can stand against a Berserker."

LEIF

The giant deer roasting for our supper did much to lift our moods. Willow stayed quiet, threading her fingers together or plucking at the pelt she wore around her shoulders. Yet, after all she'd been through, she appeared to accept her captivity.

When she picked at her food, Brokk shook his head.

"You will eat more," he commanded, spearing another portion and hovering over her, arms crossed over his chest, until she gulped it down. I hid my grin. The two of them were growing closer. It didn't matter if Brokk acted gruff and overbearing. Willow had begun to trust.

"Have an onion." I speared one and handed it to her, still on the knife. We'd found a few wild ones and roasted them in the embers.

"I'm full," she muttered, but when I shook the root at her, she took it and chewed without further argument.

"Good, lass. We'll fatten you up in no time."

She rolled her eyes, but as Brokk and I kept devouring the meat, she stretched out on the pelts, hand on her stomach, and sighed, a happy sound. My wolf felt satisfied; our mate seemed content.

"Full moon tonight," Brokk remarked.

Willow jerked and shot to her feet. Alarmed, Brokk and I half rose as well, alert for danger.

"What is it, lass?"

"The m-moon," she stammered. "I must...you must stay away."

I frowned. "Why? What is happening?"

"The fever...it takes me. I do not know what it is," she admitted. "I have prayed many times for release."

"What are the symptoms of this fever?" Brokk asked. He and I shared the same thought.

"Please don't make me tell you."

I let out a low growl, not directed at her. My wolf grew agitated, scenting her fear, and it roused the beast.

Stay calm, brother, Brokk opened his mind to me, sharing his control. Out loud he said, "Tell us, Willow."

We waited, and when the woman said nothing, he continued, "Tell us of this heat that comes over you. Do you feel it in your breast and in your cunny?"

I did not need full light to see the flush creep across her face.

She nodded.

"It's not sickness. There is nothing wrong with you, or any other woman who suffers from it. The heat is one of the reasons you are fit to be a Berserker bride. Your scent calls to us," Brokk said. "It both arouses and soothes the beast. Submit to us, and you will be well."

Her head jerked no.

"Yes." Brokk stalked behind her, blocking her escape in case she darted out of the keep and ran. "We can heal your fever."

"How?"

"We will fuck you until you cannot walk."

Willow went rigid.

I glared at Brokk. *Didn't we decide I would be the one to explain things?*

I speak the truth.

The truth comes better from a silver tongue.

I cleared my throat. "Don't fear, lass. We took an oath not to touch you before your time." *One we will uphold.*

Brokk nodded.

"What Brokk tried to tell you, lass, is whatever you need, we'll give to you. How do you wish us to help? We will do what we can to ease your suffering. We are your mates. We will see to your every need." *See, Brokk? Gentle words. Sweet tone.*

"I don't need anything from you," she said, with a spark of the fierceness I'd first noticed in her. She kept it buried, beaten-down, but it was there. She glanced behind her at Brokk cutting off her escape, and despair rose in her scent.

"No? What about the Corpse King? Do you think he would be able to resist the scent of your sweet cunt? Your heat calls to him, as it does to us."

"I'd give him a week to find you," Brokk growled.

Willow's features twisted in pain. I longed to comfort her, but we had to make her understand. "We will not let him take you. You are ours, and ours alone. But the day will come when your heat will be too much, and then you will beg us to ease it. You must."

She shook her head, her hands clenched into fists. "I hate this," she whispered, too low for us to hear. "I hate it. I hate myself."

"Come here, Willow," Brokk ordered. To my surprise, she went to him. He caught her chin between two fingers.

"You're our mate. I know you do not believe it, but soon you will know it, deep down. And we will care for you." Each word came out a command, and Willow relaxed further, her eyes growing hooded. "Tell me you understand."

"I understand," she breathed. Her body, her submissive nature responded to Brokk's orders, even if her mind struggled. His hand slid to the back of her neck, collaring the fragile stem. Her shoulder relaxed, and her breathing calmed.

My cock throbbed in my breeches. I took a deep breath, filling my lungs with her delicious scent.

"Good," Brokk almost purred. "When the heat comes on you, you will be safe. We will watch over you and make sure nothing happens."

"But—" she blurted, and stopped.

"What is it?"

She hung her head. "What I do...the way I act...it is unseemly."

Again, he tipped up her chin. "We are your mates. With us, you need not hide."

WILLOW

I sat on the wall, my arms wrapped around my knees, facing the moon. The comforting weight of the wolf pelt rested on my shoulders. Behind me, the two men sat by the fire, talking. They spoke of hunting and laying traps, and of the many birds nesting near the lake. Every once in a while, they'd pause, and my back would prickle as I felt them watching me. Grateful they kept their distance, I didn't need them to come close to make me aware of their presence. My thoughts revolved around them in endless circles.

What could I do? My body ached, wet and ready. Soon the moon would pull me into her embrace. I'd come into heat and lose all good sense.

I had to slip away. Not far. I wasn't unwise enough to try to escape and risk falling into the hands of the Grey Men. But I had to hide away for the night.

I rose and announced, "I am ready for bed."

The warriors watched me head to the pelts. Either the light played tricks, or their eyes really did glow in the moonlight.

I lay down, body throbbing. Soon my heat would take me, and I would long to fling the pelt from me and strip off my shift. I braided and rebraided a length of my hair until footsteps crunched near my head, and I forced myself to lay still.

A part of me hoped they would shift into wolves. Even though I'd been afraid of Brokk's transformation, I couldn't deny I felt more at ease around him in his canine shape. The magic had been...startling. I'd seen so many awful and shocking things since leaving the abbey, the warriors' power seemed almost comforting. They said they'd protect me, and, for some reason, I believed them.

Besides, Brokk smiled more as a wolf.

A large body lay down next to me. I fought not to stiffen. Another settled on the other side of me. They had me trapped.

The thought made me tense and excited at the same time.

"Calm, lass," Leif murmured. "We'll protect you this night."

Neither of the warriors touched me. Nor did they speak again. I kept my eyes closed, and after a time, their breathing evened.

It would be wise for me to wait, so I stayed as long as I dared. Lying there, curled up between them like a seed in a pod, I felt warm, safe. At home. But the moon rose higher with every passing second. My flesh tuned to the light, trembling with wanton energy.

The longer I lay, the more the slow, inexorable ache built in my breasts and between my legs. I could smell my musky arousal, but I no longer felt embarrassed. The warriors had stolen me from my home and insisted on keeping me. Let them suffer.

A part of me wished they hadn't sworn the oath. It would be so easy to roll either to the left or the right and tuck my arm around a broad shoulder. My lips would find theirs, delighting in the rasp of their short beards on my tender skin. They were large and heavy with muscle. I longed for the weight on top of my small form, pinning me down, grounding me, their touch both satisfying and driving me wild.

A gasp escaped my lips, unbidden. I clenched my fists, fighting not to touch between my legs. In the shed, I used to lock myself up so I could not reach my nethers. In the morning, Sage would release me, and I'd hidden the red marks on my wrists and ankles under a long-sleeved gown.

The abbey was so distant, many leagues away. My time there seemed almost a dream, and this moment, lying between two warriors, so real. I heard every breath, felt every sigh as a tremor through my own body. My senses heightened as they'd never been. The heat denied by the events of last night descended, tenfold.

When I could resist no longer, I rose and snuck away. Without glancing back to make sure the warriors were still sleeping, I climbed over the wall and dropped onto the soft green turf below. Let them wake and hunt me, if they must. I had to at least try to find privacy, and I had an idea.

Halfway to my destination, I sensed movement behind me. The warriors followed. They made no sound. Did they think I was caught in a trance, lulled by the moon? Perhaps I was.

I ignored their giant creeping shadows. Let them come. Let them watch. Let them want.

Shucking off my shift as I went, I stepped onto the shore of the lake. I'd learned to swim at the abbey, in the little pond full of mud and croaking frogs. The frogs didn't bother me as I reveled in the warm water, and the other girls stayed away.

Tonight, the water drew me, the lake a black scrying bowl reflecting the silver moon. I walked so far into the water it lapped at my waist.

"Willow," the warriors called. I stopped and waited until the ripples died away.

The water wrapped my heated body with cold drawn from the deep. The moon limned a path from me to the shore where the warriors stood. I trembled. I was an impure vessel. If I raised my arms, would the moonlight wash me clean?

The friar spoke against the religions of old, the rites of spring. A priestess would lie with a man, the warrior wearing the horns of antler, the goddess and god come together in unholy union. The friar told us this is wrong. But my thoughts returned to it again and again. I felt a deep ache in my loins, a readiness. I desired an evil, cursed ritual. What did that say about me?

"Willow, what are you doing?"

"Fighting the curse," I called across the water. My teeth chattered.

"Must you fight?"

"I must. I wish it were not like this."

"Willow." Brokk squatted on the shore. "Come to me."

"No." My plea broke from my lips even as my feet obeyed the warrior's order. No matter how brutish and awful he seemed, I couldn't resist his commands. "Please let me hide. I will lose control." I almost wept.

"No, little one. You must give in. Give yourself to us. Obey, and we will keep you safe." My tears had dried by the time I reached him. The water parted away from my naked flesh, revealing every inch. Leif still stood in the shadows. He sucked in a breath, but Brokk did not blink.

"How long have you suffered from this heat?"

"Ever since I became a woman, but it has become worse. I cannot hold back. I cannot—"

He hushed me, rising.

I realized I was shivering, not so impervious to the night chill as I'd thought. Brokk stripped off his jerkin and put it on me. It smelled of his manly musk and still held the warmth of his body. The scent would drive me mad.

"I don't know what to do," I choked out. "I cannot control it. The Corpse King will find me..."

"Willow, do you wish us to help you? Will you do as we command?"

"Yes. Anything, just help me."

"You must obey. This is important." His expression was strained. "You must not fight us," he rasped. "It entices the beast, and our control is already thin. Promise me."

"I promise."

"And you will not hide from us. We will know every thought, every fear, so we can care for you. Do you agree?"

"Yes. Please, I'm so afraid—"

"Hush," he said and wrapped his arms around me.

"Let's get her to the fire." Leif hung back, and, for once, he seemed as sober as Brokk.

Brokk carried me to the keep. He bid me sit on a pelt-draped stone near the fire. Leif kept the blaze high. He left several times and returned with more kindling. Brokk stayed close, chafing my hands and braiding back my hair.

"Tell me what happens." Brokk glanced at the moon, still high on her celestial throne. "We need to know what to expect."

"I ache." I touched my chest. "Through and through. My body grows hot. I need to find some way to cool it."

"Your scent grows enticing," Leif muttered.

Brokk waved a hand to silence his friend. "What else, Willow?"

"My breasts, my loins...everything aches with longing. I want what I should not want."

"Why do you resist?"

I shook my head. "It is not right. I must not let it control me. And yet...there are things I want."

The warriors exchanged glances.

I grew frantic. "You must not touch me. You must not."

Brokk held up a hand and I fell silent. "I give you my word, Willow. We will not touch you. Not this night, even if you beg for it."

"Thank you." I relaxed.

"Now"—he settled back a few feet from where I sat—"part your legs."

I froze.

"Do as I say, and I will keep you safe, even from yourself."

My heartbeat picked up, but I could not refuse him. His jerkin came to mid-thigh, but when I parted my legs, it drew up higher. They could see my wet center. My shame. I let out a little sob.

"Touch yourself."

"What?"

"Put your hand between your legs, as you long to do." He cocked his head to the side. "Have you never touched yourself?"

"No," I whispered. To do so was forbidden. When the friar found girls touching themselves, he locked them away. Sage and I avoided punishment because we hid.

"Do it now, Willow," Brokk ordered. "Your captors command it."

With a half-hitched breath, I hovered my hand over my throbbing center, but I could not touch it.

"This is wrong." A whine broke from my lips.

"Easy, lass. Start higher. Touch your face," Leif said. "Just a finger. Run it over your lips. Are they soft?"

"Yes."

"Now lower." Brokk's voice deepened. "Trail it down your neck, above your breasts. Now in between. Do you want to touch your nipples?"

"Yes."

"You may not. You do not have permission."

I whimpered. The stern tone in his voice made fluid gush from my cunny. My breasts throbbed, longing for attention. "You will not touch your breasts unless by our command. Soon, you will beg us to fondle them." As he spoke, my nipples grew tight.

I let out a whimper.

"You will obey, or you will be punished," Brokk said. "Now, slide your hand lower, over your belly. Between your legs. And...stop. What do you feel?"

"Wet," I answered. "Heat."

"What you are touching now belongs to us." Brokk's voice deepened to a growl. "At the abbey, you bound yourself with shackles. Now, you will obey us, or we will bind you. Do you understand?"

"Yes." My heart beat faster. I felt a responding prickle between my legs.

"Stroke yourself gently," Leif commanded. "Just the barest touch of your fingers."

"Now lift them," Brokk said, "and touch them to your tongue."

I did as he ordered, trembling. I tasted a little sweet. When I told them this, both the warriors groaned.

"All right, Willow. You're doing well." Brokk shifted a little, adjusting his breeches. His brow furrowed with concentration. "Lie on your back."

I moved as if in a trance and slid down so my bottom rested on the pelt and my head lay on the stone.

"Legs apart," Brokk rasped, "so we can see you. Rest your hand over your cunny."

At the slightest pressure, I let out a little sigh.

"You will not do this unless ordered, do you understand?" Brokk's stern tone sent tingles up and down my body.

"Yes," I breathed. I should feel frightened, carrying out this forbidden act, but I felt nothing but excitement. His orders made me strong.

"Set your legs apart," Brokk ordered. "Wider."

I did as he bid and let my hand trace the outline of my nether lips.

"Hold yourself open. Show me your wetness."

I did so and someone—maybe Leif—sucked in a breath.

"Beautiful. Continue to stroke up and down. Use two fingers."

My lower lips throb at the barest touch.

"I need—"

"Hush. We will give you what you need."

It was too much—the warriors staring at me, the deep desires of my heart, the pull of the moon. My pleasure came forth in a rush.

"I –" My words broke off with a cry.

My belly and lower back tensed. A great wave hit me, warmth spreading through me, lights flashing behind my eyes. My lower lips fluttered around my fingers, my channel aching with emptiness, longing to be filled.

"Good girl," Brokk said. He'd seated himself closer. His eyes glowed. I wanted to reach out and touch him, to feel if his skin burned as hot as mine.

"By the end of the night, you will learn to ask permission before you take your pleasure," Brokk told me. "Otherwise, you will be punished."

In a haze, I nodded.

"Good." He cleared his throat. "Now, touch yourself again."

BROKK

"She likes you," Leif said.

"She does not." I leaned against the wall, watching Willow sleep. We had ordered her to climax over and over, watching her hands on the petals of her sex. We'd exhausted her.

After she fell asleep, both of us had walked to the edge of the wall and found our own release, gasping as we painted the stones with our seed.

"She trusts you, then," Leif said. "She obeys your orders."

"She grew up with strict rules. Some shackles are in the mind."

"We must break them, then, and soon. At any moment, the Corpse King's spies might find us, but we must bond with her before we return. Claim her before we present her to the pack." Leif frowned.

"You are so sure she is ours? Maybe she is meant for another." My heart hoped otherwise, of course, but it had betrayed me. The last time I'd loved a woman, it had ended in pain.

I'd barely gotten the words out before I slammed against the stone. Leif pushed his face close to mine, his fangs out, his body ready to Change into the beast.

"She is ours," he snarled, his eyes glowing bright.

"Control," I snapped. The order came from my mind. It held him rigid until the beast receded and Leif returned. He let me go. I was breathing hard from holding myself back from attack.

"Apologies, brother," Leif panted. He waited for my tight nod before he walked away.

I sighed. My warrior brother had held out so long, his beast fighting for control. It would not do for him to lose it when we had our mate in our grasp. Leif was ruled by passion, but I'd learned long ago to guard myself from desire. I could not allow myself even the barest feeling, even though the little woman sleeping near me tugged at my heart.

LEIF

Dawn had broken by the time I returned from the hunt.

We still had meat from the last kill, but until we got Willow to accept our claim, we would be glad not to have to leave to fetch food.

The musk of her arousal still hung over the keep, and the memory of her cries... I'd had to take my cock in hand twice since she'd climaxed under the full moon, and still it felt hard as stone.

I dropped the bundle of rabbits onto a stone for cleaning and glanced about.

"Where is she?" I asked Brokk.

"In the lake. I can hear her splashing—she will not go far."

"You trust her more than I do."

He gave me a sly look. "If she disobeys she will be punished."

My cock pulsed in my breeches at that. Brokk acted stern, but I could read the eagerness he tried so hard to suppress. Let him pretend he had no feelings. He wanted the woman as much as I did. He clung to caution, but soon he would not be able to resist Willow's charms.

I trotted down to the lake and stopped short. The woman stood in the water, a nymph waiting for me. Her dark hair covered her breasts, her eyes were closed, head tipped back. I paced the shore, taking in every angle, but it took me a moment to realize she had her hand between her legs.

"Lass." My shout rang out and startled the birds on the shore.

She looked up with a start, and her climax took her. She shook, trying to hold it in, but couldn't help her squeaks of surprise.

I grinned wide. She'd broken a rule. A good thing I'd come across her, or she might not have been caught—her orgasm had been so quiet. One day I would have fun teasing her, telling her to hold back, even as I forced her climax to burst forth. On that day, she would not be able to stifle her cries.

I raised my hand and beckoned.

She came and picked up her shift, her eyes downcast. She did not seem embarrassed at her nudity anymore. A good sign. Our little woman was a wanton, even though she was dismayed by it.

I caught her chin and tilted up. "What did Brokk tell you about taking your own pleasure?"

"He said I should not," she muttered. I sensed her gathering for a fight. "I am supposed to wait for you."

"Yes," I said. "Your pleasure is for your mates to enjoy."

Her hands curled into fists at her side. I half hoped she take a swing at me. Disciplining her would be sweet.

"I have just discovered how to give myself pleasure," she said. "You will not take it from me."

"When Brokk first told you to touch yourself, what did you feel?"

"Shame," she bit out.

"And what you feel now?" She had snuck away and hid this from us. We could not let her fall back into the pattern she had at the abbey—hiding herself for fear she would not be accepted. Deep down, she wanted to be loved for who she was, lust and all. We would coax her out of her habit of fear and self-denial. "Well? What made you want to leave Brokk and I and touch yourself where you could not be seen?"

"Shame," she whispered.

"When you're with us, lass, you should only feel pleasure." I couldn't help tracing a drop of water down the slope of her breast. She shivered, and her scent grew needy.

I made her walk naked, clothes in her arms, in front of me back into the keep.

Brokk stood waiting, his arms crossed over his chest. "You tried to hide from us, Willow, when you promised not to."

"I'm sorry."

"Go to the wall." He pointed. "Set your nose against it. Stand there and wait for us to decide your punishment."

With a resigned glance at me, she did so. He approached her once to set a pelt around her shoulders and tuck her wet hair back so it would not cool her skin.

She rocked from foot to foot until Brokk gave a sharp order. "Be still."

I sucked in a breath at his harsh tone. But, in the next few minutes, the keep filled with the musk of her arousal.

She responds well to your commands.

Brokk grunted. He didn't smile, but a pleased look hovered in the corner of his mouth. Our woman would learn our rules, and she would thrive in them. When she felt comfortable with us, and embraced her life as a spaewife, we would allow her full freedom. By then, she would beg to remain our captive.

"Where are the leather ties?" he asked me then told me what else he wanted. Once we'd assembled what we needed, he called her back.

"Willow, come to me." He dropped a pelt at his feet and pointed. "Kneel here."

When she did, he leaned forward and touched her back until she arched it more then he nudged her knees wider apart until she sat gracefully displayed before him. His expression stayed stern and frightening, but Willow gazed up at him with large trusting eyes, waiting for his next command. My cock throbbed with jealousy.

Once Willow knelt the way he liked, Brokk rewarded her with a soft touch, palming her cheek.

"Soon we will return to the pack. You will accompany us. Wolves live by strict rules. There is an order, a hierarchy that keeps things running smoothly. The weaker always follows the stronger." His finger followed one lock of dark hair down to where it curled over her breast. "And, right now, who is the weaker here?"

"I am," she said.

"So, who should you obey?"

"You." Her gaze darted to me. "And Leif."

Brokk cupped her chin, drawing her attention. "I know this is new, little one, but we will learn together. For now, these will help you." He held up the bands of soft leather we had prepared. "Stand up," he said. "Close your eyes."

"What—" she started to ask, but he pinched her nipples so hard she gasped and took a step back.

I rose to my feet.

No, Leif. Brokk said without glancing at me.

Willow's chest rose and fell and her eyes were larger than ever, but she stared at Brokk, entranced.

"You asked us to help you. Will you trust me?"

She gave a slight nod, but it was enough to relax me.

"Then, do as I command," Brokk murmured.

I watched, fascinated, as she stepped back to where she had been and closed her eyes.

Brokk held out his hand, and I came forward with the rest of the soft leather ties. Together, we would bind our bride the way we wished.

The first leather strap wrapped under her breasts, the soft leather encircling her narrow rib cage. It crossed over and under and back again until she wore a harness that supported her breasts and lifted them to our gaze. Her nipples were small, tight pink buds on the beautiful pale orbs.

"Lovely," Brokk murmured.

Willow let out a shuddering sigh.

"I smell your arousal," I told her, running a finger down her back. "It pleases me." Goose bumps rose on her bottom as I stroked it. "So smooth and soft." I cupped between her legs, and she leaned into my touch, making a low noise in her throat.

Brokk cleared his throat. I stepped back, but not before I pinched her fleshy backside. It was the perfect size for my large hand to caress, or smack. More than anything, I wanted to mark the pale skin, make it red.

Brokk checked the straps wrapped around her naked torso and sat back on his heels. "What do you think, Leif?"

"She is lovely. A beautiful rose," I declared, and my warrior brother almost rolled his eyes. Willow glowed, her cheeks pink. "So beautiful, especially when she obeys. Still, she defied our commands. We must uphold our vow to guide her. Punishment is in order, don't you think?"

"Yes." Brokk picked up more leather straps. "But, first, another binding. Widen your stance." He touched Willow and helped her move her feet more than shoulder length apart. This time, the straps went around each leg, and wound around her hips over and over, making a harness to frame her mound. The final strips ran from the center of the hip brace, between her legs. The soft leather pressed right between her fleshy, lower lips, plump and shiny with her sticky arousal. Willow's breathing picked up. Her hands curled into fists, her thighs tensing as Brokk brushed her sensitive area again and again.

"Put your hands on your head," Brokk ordered, and she did. The position lifted her breasts beautifully.

When he finished, she had a harness about her hips as well as her chest, a makeshift belt that would both keep her from touching herself, and torment her. With every movement, the leather slid along her slit, growing dark and slippery.

"You may open your eyes and look if you wish," Brokk said.

Her breath shortened as she studied the bindings. Her lips parted, but she did not take her hands from her head. She stayed restrained by the rope and our will. My cock felt so hard, it took all my control not to fall to my knees and spill on the ground.

I choked down a whine. Brokk kept a firm hold on his desires, testing the straps solemnly. Willow leaned towards him, hungry for touch.

"How do you feel?" he asked.

"I want to touch, but now I cannot."

"This will remind you who owns you. Who cares for you and keeps you safe."

Her shoulders relaxed.

"Now, lass." I seated myself on a stone and beckon. "Come here. You're in for punishment."

I tugged at the leather bindings, making her breath catch. "Your mates are able to pleasure you, but you cannot. We will bind your hands if you do it again. Keep you hobbled all day."

"Even when we are back with the pack?"

"Even then. For it is understood that a Berserker will train his mate any way he pleases. As long as he cherishes her and does not do her harm."

Brokk gave a nod.

"Now." I guided her over my legs, keeping her off-balance. With no trouble, I supported her little body, liking how her small fingers clutched at my legs. My hands cupped her bottom. The bindings left the rounded portion of her bottom bare.

"A hundred on each cheek sounds fair, right?"

Willow gave up a cry of protest, and Brokk laughed.

"Leif jests," he assured her. "Although the next time you touch, we will not be so lenient."

"I'll spank her until her cheeks are pink as a rose." I squeezed her bottom and swatted it, watching color rise to the surface. "It should not be long. Perhaps she will even enjoy it." I put my hand between her legs. Sure enough, she grew wet, squirming. Every bit of her struggle would make the leather straps rub between her legs.

I increased the force of my slaps, covering every inch of her exposed buttocks. In no time, she cried out with every slap, but her cunt grew slick, the scent of her arousal rising in a thick miasma over her reddened bottom. When I stopped, she shook on the edge of a climax.

"Will you touch yourself without permission?"

"No, no," she said.

I positioned her so her mound rubbed right against my knee.

She gasped. "Please, please. I will not touch. I will be good."

"Do you need permission to climax?" Brokk squatted in front of her, moving her hair from her face. "Be honest."

"I—" She hung her head. "I should not want this."

"You are in heat," he reminded. "You have needs. It is our job to see to them."

"Then, yes." She hung her head. "I want this."

Brokk gave me a nod and I turned her over, cradling her on my lap. I hooked her legs outside of my knees. "Keep your legs spread," I whispered, and nipped her earlobe. She melted into me.

"You did well for your first punishment. I hope to punish you many, many more times. I think you like it."

"No," she breathed. I put my hand between her legs. The leather felt slippery. "Did you just lie to me?" Pressing down, I rubbed, making the leather slide between her folds. "No," she squealed before a moan stole her breath.

"Lying deserves more punishment," Brokk said. "Here." He came forward with two small ties and wound them about her nipples after he pinched them tight. "We require honesty at all times. This will help you remember." Willow's breath came in short pants. Her climax hovered close.

"And now for the final part of your punishment." I smacked between her legs with enough force to jar her pussy. She stiffened but did not cry out. I did it again. This time, her breath left in a rush. She planted her feet and pushed up, trying to get as far away as she could. My arm banded around her middle, holding her against me. I ground her against my erection. Her soft bottom molded to it, and I moaned. "Soon, we will take you," I told her in a harsh whisper. "We will not be able to hold back. But, now, you will come for us." I swatted her again and cupped her puffy mound. It throbbed under my hand. With my palm, I rubbed her slippery flesh, grinding the straps deeper into the pink valley of her folds. I alternately tugged the straps and pressed on her aroused flesh.

Her body tensed, arching like a drawn bow.

"Take your pleasure." My slick fingers pulled the straps so they lay alongside her sensitive nub, exposing the tiny piece of erect flesh. I slapped her cunt three times, until it was pink and needy. I thumbed the small erect bud, brushing it as carefully as I would a flower petal. Willow moaned, a sound between agony and ecstasy.

"Leif..."

I pinched the tiny nub. "Now, lass." A wail tore from her throat. Her legs tensed, her hips rocking, pulsing like her empty cunt as she came.

I wrapped her tight in my arms, almost crushing her. Holding her, holding in my own fierce desire, lest her cries break me apart. My cock had turned into a rock under her twitching ass. Her needy sounds went on and on. She twitched, sweat rolling between the straps crisscrossing her body. Her climax carried her so far, it would take a long time for her to come to herself. I would hold her as long as she needed. Forever, if that's what it took.

"Shh, Willow." Brokk hovered over her. He held a waterskin to her lips, and I cradled her as she drank. She was still groggy with pleasure, trusting us to hold her together until then. I felt satisfied. It had given me great pleasure to break her apart.

"How was that?" Brokk asked, setting down the waterskin.

She bobbed her head, still too overcome to speak.

Gold light gleamed in his eyes.

He rubbed himself through his leather pants. "Do you want to thank your captors for their kindness to you?"

She nodded again, frantically.

There it is, I sent to Brokk. *The submission, the longing.*

We must be careful not to take her when her mind is altered.

But I scoffed. *She wants it.* I set her on her knees.

"Are you sure, Willow?" Brokk came to stand in front of us.

"Please," she choked out, reaching for him.

"Oh no." I caught her hands behind her back and held them there. "Use only your mouth."

She moaned again, and I nearly came at the sound.

Brokk took himself out, his cock as angry-looking and turgid as mine. "Just kisses," he told her. "Be gentle."

"No teeth," I added.

Frantic little moans escaped her throat, the sexiest sounds I'd ever heard. I teased her hair back as she kissed and licked Brokk's cock.

"This is a gift," he told her. "You are only allowed this once you please us."

"I'll give you a gift every morning and evening, lass." I stroked her hair. "I am a generous man."

Brokk's face tensed as he fought not to come in her mouth.

With impressive control, he stepped back. "You will learn to take me in your mouth. For now, just watch." He stroked himself before her until he spent his cum on the ground. "You have not yet earned my seed."

Willow licked her lips, and I couldn't help myself. I gripped a handful of her dark hair and drew her to face me.

"My turn." I wanted her hands, though. I stayed seated and let her explore. She touched my turgid shaft and the sac hanging below it.

"Ahh, lass. We will never let you go."

She gave me a small, quick smile. My cum boiled in my balls. My toes curled. "Now, lass, you've been so good, I will allow you to take it in your mouth."

Willow nodded and sucked the head. My hips surged up, but I caught myself in time, barely keeping from fucking her face.

"You have a wicked mouth," I told her. "Devil-blessed."

She drew off with a pop. The hard sucking action made me spurt. I splashed onto her face as she sat there, blinking.

I swept my thumb across her cheek and fed some to her.

"You did well." I smiled. "I think we will keep you."

Brokk came with a cloth to wipe her face. He unbound her gently, washing the sweat off her slick body and rubbing the marks the bonds had made.

"You did well," he repeated. She reached for him, but he rose, cast a glance my way. "Leif will tend to you."

When he walked off, she watched him go.

WILLOW

My muscles ached as Brokk strode from the keep. Leif wet a pelt and washed himself before tucking his cock in his pants. I kept my head averted, blinking back tears.

"Willow? What's wrong, lass?"

"Nothing."

"Do not hide from me. We will not punish you for honesty."

"I gave in. I was weak." Brokk did not want to be seen with such a wanton creature. Hunching my shoulders, I hid my face. "Please, leave me."

Setting the wet pelt aside, he gathered me in his arms. "Do you know why we torment and tease you?"

"Because you like it."

His fingers trailed down my legs. "Are we the only ones?"

I twisted in his grip, but he held me fast.

"Let's check, shall we?" His fingers found my cunny and dipped inside. "You're close aren't you, sweet rabbit?"

My head thrashed against his shoulder. I tried to free myself, but he gripped me harder and somehow kept his hand between my legs, light touches pushing me towards the cliff edge.

"Please..."

He showed me his glistening fingers. "Do you know what this makes you?"

I shut my eyes and waited for him to say it. *Dirty, wanton, wrong.*

"Perfect. It makes you perfect."

His fingers delved deep, calling my climax with a come-hither motion. He held me as I went over.

When I finally stilled, Leif took my wrist and bound it to his with leather ties.

"We will sleep," he said. "Unless you are not yet sated." The moonlight glinted off his yellow eyes.

"I am.... satisfied. Thank you, Leif." We lay down, and the giant warrior tucked me against his body. This was what I'd always wanted. A man's hard muscled chest under my cheek, his fingers playing over my back. A warrior ready to protect me from the world.

I shivered.

"Cold?" He pulled a pelt over us.

"No." I raise my head. "Does Brokk not like me?"

Leif sighed and propped his head up on his arm. I wanted him to keep touching me but dared not ask.

"Brokk's always been an odd sort. Satisfied with being a lone wolf even before we were Changed."

"How did you two meet?"

Leif grimaced. "We fought over a woman."

My eyes widened.

"That was a long time ago," Leif said with a forced laugh. "I'm sure he's forgotten it." But he did not sound so sure.

"You say I am your mate. Will you share me?" I traced the smooth dip between the powerful muscles of his chest.

"Thinking of mating us?"

I nodded, shy.

"Oh, lass," he groaned. "You don't know how enticing you are."

I was relieved to see the easiness return to his handsome face. Even if Brokk had left, Leif and I could share a moment.

"Brokk and I are bound together with an unbreakable bond. We saved each other's lives and kept each other alive over these years while we waited for you."

"Can the bond break?"

"Only in a fit of madness. That is why we fear the beast. What gives us strength is also our greatest weakness." His fingers slipped under the pelt to swirl again over my bare back. I held my breath, willing him not to stop. "When the time comes, we will take you fully, and you will belong to us forever. Your submission allows the beast to rule peacefully, its hunger sated on your flesh."

"And Brokk will stay with us?"

He frowned. "We will share you. The three of us will be linked."

"He does not seem to want me."

"He is afraid of caring for someone. Long ago, the people he cared about betrayed him."

THAT NIGHT, I dreamed I stood on the shore of the lake. The moon cut a silver trail over the endless black water. I stepped forward and instead of sinking, I walked over the watery expanse as easily as I would dry land. My feet carried me to an island I hadn't noticed before, emerging from the mist in the center of the lake.

When I arrived on the shore, something drew me on. I walked to the center of the island, pushing through the small bushes and ferns. A willow tree leaned over a circle of stones. I stood among them, turning slowly, wondering at the feeling I had been there before.

∽

When I woke, the sunlight shone across my face. My loins ached from last night's climaxes, my lower lips puffy and well used.

"Up you come, lass," Leif called. "You slept half the day away."

I stretched. I'd grown used to my captivity. The days spent with these wild but gentle warriors. A strange new life, but I did not mind it anymore.

"Come," Leif repeated. "There are apples for breakfast. Let's get you fed and washed. Brokk has brought you something."

He took me to the lake and rinsed me well. I pressed my face against his fine chest, blushing. My flushed cheeks seemed to fascinate him. His fingers played over them, and I kissed them. Too late, I realized he was naked. His cock brushed my thigh and set me aching again.

"Leif," I breathed.

His thumb brushed over my mouth, but he drew away and washed himself while I went back to shore.

Remembering my dream, I paused and squinted, but, even in the bright day, I could not make out an island.

When we returned, a pile of new items lay on a large rock.

"What's this?" I asked when Leif handed me a jug.

"Mead."

"I went to market," Brokk said. He sat on a nearby rock, watching me. Not for the first time, I admired his broad shoulders, the powerful arms and torso, the rough fingers that bound me so cleverly last night. The memory made my cheeks heat.

Leif held up an overdress I could wear over my shift.

"It's beautiful. For me?"

"It won't fit me." Leif laughed. "Nor these." He passed me a pair of small boots, lined with soft squirrel fur. I held them, too overcome to speak. The rich cloth matched the color of an oak leaf in summer, and they were lined in silk. The needlework was as neat as Sage's, and golden threads shone amid the green.

"Is this—?"

"Cloth of gold," Brokk grunted, and I clutched the garment tighter, lest I drop it. I'd never seen such finery, much less touched it.

"Put it on," Brokk ordered. "I will give you the rest of your gift."

My heart overflowed with happiness as Leif helped me dress.

When I finished, he touched my face. "Beautiful," he said, but he didn't mean my dress.

Brokk called me over. He had a pelt at his feet. I knelt before him like a fine lady come to the church altar. Leif took off his arm ring and handed it to the stern-faced warrior before lifting my hair, and letting Brokk fit the band around my neck.

"There. Now you will remember you belong to us."

I rose, and Brokk caught my hand. "Not so fast. There is one more gift."

"It is less a gift to you than a gift to us," Leif murmured.

Brokk held up a metal circle, large enough to fit around my hips. Another half circle attached.

"What's that?" I asked.

"Raise your skirts." he said. Puzzled, I did, but once he lay the metal harness on the ground and motioned for me to step into it, I realized his intent.

"Oh no." I dropped my skirts and backed away. "No, no, no."

"You do not like your gift?" Leif caught me as I backed away, his arm banded under my breasts.

"I do not want to wear that thing," I said.

The warriors did not give me a choice. Brokk knelt while Leif lifted me. My legs went through the holes, and the metal circle wrapped around my waist cinched tight. The piece running between my legs covered my sex. I could move easily and freely but could not touch my nether lips.

"How long must I wear this?" I asked.

"Until you learn not to touch. I ran to a village and woke the blacksmith. He spent all night crafting it to your measurements and smoothing the edges."

The belt fit perfectly.

"You should be grateful," Brokk told me. "This will keep you from touching. You will have control."

My thanks felt heavy on my tongue. It seemed they were mocking me, dressing me like a fine lady, harnessing me like a slave.

"Would you rather the leather strips?"

"No." I shuddered, remembering how they cut into my throbbing folds, binding and heightening my arousal at the same time.

"Come. There is something we wish to show you."

IF ANY MAN or beast had been out on the green hills around the abandoned keep, they would've seen a strange sight—a young woman in the garment of a queen walking between two warriors almost twice as tall as she. Under the beautiful dress, the metal belt did not chafe, though I had to beg to be let out to relieve myself. By the time we reach our destination, my cheeks glowed bright red, and not from too much sun.

We crested a hill, and I gasped. A purple cape spread over the land, as far as the eye could see. Acres and acres of wildflowers.

"The bonnie heather," Leif murmured. "On the rockiest soil, the goddess grew a carpet fit for a queen."

Brokk rolled his eyes. "Come, Willow. Time to break in those boots."

Leif held out his hand. "Let's run."

My heart thumped as I put my hand in his.

The redheaded warrior and I raced between the flower patches. Soon, we were laughing, skipping, dancing like crazy folk.

Brokk followed, and when I grew tired and went to sit with him, he pointed out the birds, the little rabbits, and mice who made their home in the fragrant heather. Leif dug in a pack and handed out dried meat, cheese, hard little apples. When I'd nibbled to his satisfaction, he let me have a little mead.

The day seemed endless, stretched out under a blue sky.

"Why are we here?" I asked.

"Are you not enjoying yourself?" Leif countered. "Perhaps we need a new game."

"All right," I said slowly, not liking the mischievous look on his face.

"I think it's time we gave you a chance to escape."

"What?"

"Unless, of course, you'll admit you don't want to go."

I glanced at Brokk, but he remained solemn, his arms crossed over his chest.

"Brokk, will you play with us?" Leif called to him.

"This doesn't sound like a game."

"Oh, it is. And there's a bonnie prize for the winner."

"Do you mean you will let me escape?" My heart beat hard. For some reason, I felt anxious at the thought of leaving the warriors. I should be relieved, but I was not, and that only troubled me more.

"Let you *try* to escape," Leif corrected. "We will give you a head start, but don't doubt that we will easily track you. Whoever catches you first, gets a kiss."

"And if I win?"

"You will not. But if you manage to elude us until sundown, we will throw away the metal belt."

Brokk snorted.

"Or"—Leif raised a finger—"you admit to us now that you no longer want to escape. We will remove the belt and reward you for telling the truth."

I gnawed my lip.

"I didn't think so." Leif chuckled. He rose, and I scrambled to my feet. "I call this game 'wolves and rabbit.' You're the rabbit, Willow." He packed our lunch away and lifted the horn. "We will sit and drink the rest of this mead, and then we will be on the hunt." His eyes glittered. "If I were you, I would run."

My heart beat louder than my footfalls on the soft turf. I made for a stand of boulders, hoping they would hide me. Once I passed them, I changed course, heading down a ravine. A brook ran between the rocks. I paused for a moment. The water would wash away my scent, confuse them, but it would soak my new clothes.

Behind me, an eerie howl rose from the hills. The hunt had begun.

I raced to the stream and followed it. The water soon soaked my garments and weighted me down, but I kept running. The bushes grew larger here. I could hide. I made the mistake of glancing behind me and caught sight of a muscled figure following me. The warriors must have stripped before starting the hunt. They flowed down the side of the hill, coming faster than I believed possible. Their forms seemed taller, misshapen somehow. I caught a flash of fur as if they were between the forms of man and wolf.

I couldn't outrun them. I threw myself under a prickly bush and hoped for the best.

The crunch of footsteps came closer.

I darted up, flushed from my hiding place like a desperate bird. One of them growled behind me, and I ran smack into the other.

"Got you, little Willow," Brokk breathed in my ear.

I screamed, kicking and fighting as he bore me to the ground. Leif had laid a pelt down to cushion my body, but I still struggled. Brokk turned me to my back, roughly, and I calmed somewhat, seeing their handsome faces. They now looked like men, but I'd never forget the sight of them hunting me down in the shape of a wolfish monster.

"You wet your lovely boots," Leif said.

"No matter," Brokk rasped. "Take them off."

They stripped me quickly but with care.

"What now?" I was trembling, frightened and excited at the same time.

"You lost, sweetheart. You owe us a kiss."

I nodded and moved towards Brokk. He caught my hair

in his fist. With a firm but gentle grip, he guided my head down. "Not on my mouth, sweet lass. On my cock."

I unlaced his breeches. Humming with pleasure, I took him down to the root, my tongue lapping the underside.

"Odin's staff," Brokk cursed. I grinned to myself.

"Good lass." Leif chuckled.

Brokk did his best to hold off, while I did everything I could think of to tempt him. My small hands grasped his giant thighs, holding him captive as my mouth worked over him.

In the end, he spurted so much seed, some dribbled out of my mouth. He wiped it up with his thumb and fed it to me.

"Well done," Leif said.

Brokk kissed my forehead. I glowed with pride.

"Now." Leif tugged a lock of my hair. "It is my turn to kiss you."

I turned on my knees, but Leif eased me down, my back on the pelt, my head in Brokk's lap.

"I need this belt off," Leif muttered. Brokk helped him lift me and slide it off. I gasped as the cool air hit my wet nethers.

"She's a bit cold," Brokk observed, toying with one of my pointed nipples.

Leif draped my dress over me and dove under it, between my legs.

"What—" I cried out as he kissed the inside of my thigh. His lips worked up towards my pulsing cunny. My legs strained to close, but he held them down. I panted, ready to climax by the time his mouth reached its destination. Brokk restrained me as I writhed, helpless under Leif's lashing tongue. My heels dug into the ground, back and belly tightening with pleasure. I moaned his name as I came. Once I relaxed, he emerged, wiping his mouth.

"Good game, lass. Shall we play again?"

We played "wolves and rabbit" for the rest of the afternoon. I never got to be a wolf. The stakes grew higher, and, after a time, they made me play naked. As soon as I got away from one, the other would catch me, grope me, and kiss my mouth until I gasped.

Once, I refused to run.

"Spank her and put her back in the belt," Leif suggested, and Brokk tipped me over his knees, turning my bottom red before locking me up. Then he tied my arms around my back and made me march to where Leif waited with the pack.

"We should bind your legs, too," Leif laughed. "So you have to hop, like a real rabbit."

"No." Brokk ran his hand over my bare flesh. "She might hurt herself."

They had me kneel and fed me their cocks again then had me eat more meat and apples. I sat first on Leif's, and then Brokk's lap. For all Brokk's concern, his fingers were merciless, running up and down from my hips to my breasts, tugging my nipples, kissing my neck, and nuzzling me with his stubble-roughened face.

"Please," I said when Brokk fondled the slippery flesh around the metal belt.

Again, the warriors released the belt and laid me down on the springy heather.

"You will not touch yourself. Only we may touch," Brokk

told me, and explored each curve and crevice until I writhed and shivered with pleasure.

A smile crossed his stone face when he brought a glistening hand to his mouth and licked his fingers clean.

"My turn." Leif put his mouth between my legs. My hands dug into his hair until Brokk pried them free and held my wrists down.

Pleasure blossomed, crested, broke. My cries rang out over the heather.

Once Leif finished licking me clean, they tied the belt back in place.

"Your taste is pleasing to me." Leif wiped his mouth. "Now that we know your scent, you can never run from us. We will track you as easily as a hare over deep snow."

Body humming with pleasure, I did not protest. I no longer wanted to escape these warriors.

"What will it be like being your mate?" I asked.

"Our minds will link. You'll connect with us through the bond." He touched my forehead. "You will hear us speak to you here. You'll never be able to hide your feelings from us. The three of us will be closer than any other persons on earth. We will share you, forever."

At this, Brokk rose and walked away.

Leif frowned. "Let us return."

BROKK

You should not leave us like that, Leif lectured in my head. *She thinks you do not want her.*

I have not yet decided if I do, brother. I spat the final word.

Leif stayed silent so long, I wished he'd speak and distract me from my painful thoughts.

It was so long ago, he said. *I thought you had forgiven me.*

I stepped into the forest near the keep to watch Leif and Willow return. She acted nothing like the woman I had loved back in the north lands. She'd never been touched by any other man.

And never will be, Leif said, *but we will share her equally.*

She likes you better.

You are not handsome when you sulk. Try smiling. Leif slammed the bond shut.

He took Willow down to the lakeshore while I chopped wood. They stripped naked, and their delighted shouts followed the sound of splashing. Her laughter wafted up to the keep. I threw my axe down. Willow, laughing. A few days, and Leif had wooed her, as he intended. Perhaps, tonight, he would lie with her and mark her as his mate. My heart ached as I thought about it. It would be better if he and I had not bonded. Then he could claim her for himself, and they could be happy.

Magic rippled through me at the jealous, desolate thought. The beast, clawing to the surface, ready to fight for what it wanted. It would not allow me to relinquish my mate. It wanted her just as much as Leif did.

I left. Traveling at Berserker speed, I reached the craggy heights well before dusk. The day was clear and fine, and I could see for leagues and leagues. A fog lined the southern horizon, but it was still a long way off.

In the high places, I sometimes found it easier to link to the pack. I reached out, traipsing over the cold stones to find the best place to reach them.

After climbing a tall, slender finger of rock, I caught a familiar echo.

Svein?

Brokk? Where are you?

I sent him a picture of the rocky cliffs and the ruined keep where we'd made camp. *What of you and Dagg? Are you home?*

We are hiding. The Grey Men...escaped them... The Alphas ordered...protect the women... Corpse King's magic...blocking the pack bonds...

His voice wavered in and out, but I heard enough.

I am glad you and Dagg are safe. We also met some Grey Men. I did not add how Leif nearly lost control when he called on the Berserker rage and destroyed them. *The Corpse King's magic swept through the village and turned the men into his undead servants. That is why there were so many, so quickly.*

Too many to fight...avoid them. The Alphas consult the witch to find a spell...the mage grows stronger...

We are safe, for now. We took the woman Willow, and we will keep her safe. Svein?

Yes?

I couldn't keep a smile off my face. *Have you found your mate?*

This time, his message came through clearly. *Yes. She is with us now.* He sounded proud and tender at the same time. *She was frightened, at first, but is very brave. And you?*

We have a woman. I fought to keep glee out of my voice. *Leif thinks she is the one for us.* And so did I, I realized. Otherwise, it would not bother me so much to leave or feel I must compete with Leif for her affection.

What of Rolf and Thorbjorn? I asked.

We have not heard from them. Like us, they may have traveled far to keep their mate safe, or they may be lost. The Alphas don't know.

And the woman they took?

Her name is Sage.

I felt as if someone had struck me. Sage was Willow's closest friend. I wanted to deliver good news to Willow.

Thank you for the news, I told Dagg. *Can you reach the Alphas? Tell them we are well?*

Yes. Their orders are for all of us to make our way to the mountain, but do not engage the Grey Men. Stay safe. Keep together and, whatever you do, watch over your mate.

We will. At all costs. May the moon smile on you.

When I cut off the link from my fellow Berserker, my head throbbed with pain. My beast surged to the fore, giving me strength. I pushed it back, unwilling to risk letting it loose. Staying away from the pack this long was dangerous. Without the Alphas' stabilizing strength, Leif and I must rely on one another.

I had been wrong, I realized, as I loped down the mountain. Willow belonged to me and Leif. I needed to woo her as he did, so she would laugh and smile with me.

Of course, I didn't have that skill. When I tried and failed, would she turn from me and find solace in Leif's arms?

The thought struck me like a dagger. I gritted my teeth.

As I left the mountain, I walked right into a thick mist at the foot of the high rocks. The fog I'd seen creeping up from the south had moved faster than I expected.

Brokk. Brother. Where are you?

Coming. I picked up my pace to outrun the mist.

A full moon rose above my head. I should've been excited to claim my woman with my warrior brother.

Instead, I felt only dread.

LEIF

Willow sat by the fire, a flush on her pretty cheeks from a long day in the sun. She wore a small pink rose tucked behind her ear—a gift from me. We spent every moment together, and it would be the best day of my life, bar one detail. Brokk was not there.

My head ached from our separation. I sensed he climbed high where the air grew thin and used much of his energy and reserves to reach out to the Alphas.

He came running, trying to outdistance the strange mist sweeping over the ground. I open the bond and lent him strength.

Come quickly, Brokk. We need you. I've managed to keep the beast at bay, but I will need to claim Willow soon. We both will. Why were you gone so long?

You seemed to be enjoying the day well enough without me.

Brother, how many times do I need to tell you? Together, we are stronger.

Silence. I took a deep breath and continued. *In the past century, we have come together to share many things. But I do not forget the woman who tore us apart.*

You betrayed me.

I have asked forgiveness. I have tried to atone. I am your brother and fellow warrior. I will always stand by your side.

Brokk's answer was grudging. *We are warriors, comrades in arms.*

What about Willow? You know as well as I we must both claim her. Our hold on the beast is too weak. She can heal us. You leave, and it is not fair to Willow.

No, it is not fair to her.

Let her be the bond between us. I sent him an image of our woman, curled up near me, the fine green gown drawing out the color of her eyes. Her rosy cheeks, pale skin, and wealth of dark hair. Add to that her courage, her smiles, and her scent, and she became irresistible.

For once, I did not need a silver tongue or my charm. She could convince my warrior brother to fulfill his destiny, in a way I could not.

Brokk finally answered. *If I agree, then you must promise this: we will share her equally or not at all.*

I cannot slice her down the middle with my sword.

No. But you will claim her one way, and I another.

I expected him to cut off our connection, and when he did, I went to the wall and waited until his shadow moved over the grass. His control remained strong. He'd outrun the fog and stopped to make a kill. I'd hoped he'd eat with us, he and I feeding Willow bits of choice meat, proving to her we could provide for her. But since he had fed, I left Willow and met him before he stepped into the circle of the fire.

"Brokk, when you say we will both claim her—"

He produced a carved wooden plug, shaped like a bulb, with a narrow stem flaring out again. Another item he'd commissioned at the village, no doubt.

"Willow," he called. She startled and rose to her feet, a

trace of eagerness in her step when he beckoned to her. Brokk planted his hand on the center of my chest and pushed me out of the way. I growled and staggered back. My beast rose up fighting, and I took a moment to compose myself, leaning against the wall in the shadows.

She is not ready, I said. *We must be gentle.*

"Willow, I have another gift for you."

"What is it?" she asked and touched the polished wooden piece Brokk held out to her.

"It goes in your arse," Brokk said.

She flushed and jerked her hand back.

I glared at him. *You could be kinder.*

Why, Leif?" he said out loud. "Don't you prefer when I am harsh? I train her to our will, but when the discipline is over, she runs into your arms so she cares for you, but not for me. I think this is your plan."

Willow's gaze darted between us, lines creasing her forehead.

"Fool." My voice sounded choked, guttural. Brokk had to realize I grew close to losing control. I clenched my fists and fought to keep my wits about me. Already my fingernails lengthened, curving into claws, and magic tingled up my spine, ready for the Change. "You're the one who chooses to be rude. You're the one who pushes us away."

Brokk turned his back. "Come, Willow. It is time to test your devotion to us."

"Brother, be gentle with her."

Be silent. You wanted me back, I am here. You will stand aside while I bring her to the gates of ecstasy, and beyond. His hand dropped to her bottom and squeezed it through the dress. The woman's sound of breathy surprise made my cock harden.

She wants this. She wants my dominance. It is I who sate her, not you.

My vision goes dark for a moment, fur sprouting from my arms as the magic takes hold. I push back against the wall, fighting for the upper hand. *We are to be equals in this, Brokk.*

Equals? I am not the one who cannot rule my beast. Perhaps I should take her far from here and leave you, the lonely king of the ruined keep.

I snarled and laughed from the shadows. Brokk pushed Willow forward and whirled to face me. His axe sliced up towards me. I ducked and caught his arm. The two of us grappled, equally matched in height, weight, and strength. A fight between us would not go well, and we both knew this. We glared at each other, locked in a tense embrace.

"Stop," Willow shouted. "Both of you, stop." Her voice rang out, a slight tremor in her words. "Don't fight." She stepped close, acting braver than I liked.

"Be off with you, lass," I grunted. "'Tis dangerous."

"You won't hurt me," she snapped.

After a breath, Brokk and I released each other and stepped back. Willow moved between us.

"What is it you want from me?" she asked Brokk.

"Everything. Your submission. Your cries, your pleas, your will bent to mine."

"To us," I corrected.

She nodded. "Very well."

"Lass—"

"I'm fine, Leif." She held out her hand for the plug. "I'll do it."

WILLOW

"I will do it." I repeated.

"Go to the furs," Brokk said, without taking his eyes off Leif. "Strip and kneel on the blanket. All fours."

"Arse in the air," Leif added.

Both warriors eased their stance a little but didn't take their eyes away from the other, their warrior training too ingrained for them to ignore a present threat. I gulped but hurried to do Brokk's bidding. It seemed my obedience was the only thing keeping them from tearing each other apart.

My heart thumped. What had made them fight? What would happen to me if they became enemies? Did Brokk realize his answer when I asked what he wanted of me matched Leif's? *Everything,* they'd said. These men wanted everything I had to give. They would accept nothing less. They would require nothing more.

I laid aside the beautiful garments they had given me, shivering with anticipation. My flesh glowed in the moonlight as I crossed the keep. Was I pretty enough for them? A prickle up my spine told me they watched me, and when I risked a glance back at them, it seemed they could not tear their gaze away. Their golden eyes shone with that eldritch light.

Kneeling, I settled into position, pushing my bottom into the air.

"Good girl," Brokk said, and I quivered with pleasure just from his approval.

I chewed my lip as I waited with haunches exposed, knees cushioned by the pelt. My hair fell over my face, until one of the warriors knelt beside me and tucked it back. Leif. His face had lost the strain of the past few moments, but he didn't seem his jovial, joking self. He ran a thumb over my lips. I closed my lips over it, sucking as I'd pleasured his cock the night before. His gaze turned heated, and one corner of his mouth turned up in a smile by the time he took his hand away. I relaxed further. It frightened me more than I wanted to admit when the rage had taken over his charming face. Brokk, I expected to be stern, standoffish. I'd thought I'd broken through his armor, but their fight shook me.

Perhaps I did have something to give these warriors. My sweetness and surrender and acceptance of whatever they would do. So far, every experience they brought me gave me great pleasure. I trusted them. They had not failed me yet.

Brokk's hand gusted over my backside.

"Lovely," he murmured.

"We have no oil to ease the plug's passage," Leif said. "What will you use?"

"Her own juices." Brokk's fingers touched between my legs. He stroked my puffy lower lips. "Did you wear the belt all afternoon?"

"Yes, Brokk," I told him.

"Did it make you feel owned, Willow? Did you ache and think of me?"

"Yes." My head hung lower. With the belt locked around my loins, every time my cunny throbbed in pleasure, I remembered them putting their creation on me, guarding my sex from anyone's touch but their own. And, every time I thought of it, I ached all over again.

"Leif is lenient. He freed you after a few hours. I would have you wear it all day and all night. Touching you would be my privilege, and mine alone. I'd remove the belt to clean and inspect you, and each time, I'd heat the water and run the cloth over every inch of your skin. When I washed between your legs, I would take care, and go ever so slowly. And if you came, you would be punished." He pinched one of my lips, and I sucked back my squeal. His voice was hushed, reverent, as if he'd slipped into a trance. I did not want to break the spell.

"So wet, so ready," Brokk continued. "There's plenty of honey here to use to penetrate your bottom."

"Get on with it, then," Leif grunted, but he didn't sound angry, just eager. He knelt beside me, his cock right by my head, pressing against his breeches. I lifted my hand and traced it with a teasing finger. He caught my wrist and lifted my hand to his mouth to suck on my fingertip. His canines grazed my skin and I whimpered.

"Steady, lass. We have a long way to go." Brokk ran a wet cloth between my bottom cheeks, pressing it into my small hole. The intimate probing had me hanging my head in embarrassment.

"Nothing to be ashamed of," Leif said. "Your mates will tend to you and clean you inside and out."

I sucked in a breath as Brokk dipped his fingers between

my nether lips, gathering the moisture there and painting the area around my bottom hole. His fingertip pushed at my pucker, and I clenched.

"Easy," Brokk crooned. His tender tone surprised me. Exhaling, I opened to him, and his finger slipped inside. He worked me a little, stretching the edges, playing with the rim of my crinkled hole.

"Isn't she beautiful?" Brokk breathed. I blinked at Leif, who winked back, his smile returned in full force. The hard armor Brokk wore had fallen away, and revealing the passionate man underneath. Leif always displayed his feelings, but Brokk hid them away like a treasure for me to find. I loved both, but I savored this glimpse of the man Brokk could be.

"Oh yes, she's very wet. She likes this."

"No," I whined, and a hand laid a heavy swat on my right buttock.

"Be good," Leif reminded me.

"This is not right," I protested. My face felt hot. I wished I could shake my hair down and hide behind its screen.

Leif cupped my chin. "You trust your mates. We do this for your own pleasure and ours."

"I bet she could take her pleasure from stimulation here." Brokk's finger pushed into my back hole. The stimulation made the muscles of my cunny flutter, begging to be filled.

"Oh aye."

As Brokk's digit fucked my arsehole, a curl of arousal wound through me, a lazy loop that tightened my muscles, heralding my climax.

Brokk kept teasing my back hole as his thumb brushed between my nether lips again, collecting more juices.

"Oh no." My mouth went slack, my legs trembling.

Brokk's touch didn't bother me as much as the thought I could climax just from this indecent stimulation. "No." I put my head down lower, hiding my face.

"Be good, Willow," Leif said. "Be a good girl."

Something hard and unyielding probed my bottom. Brokk fucked me slowly with the plug, stretching the ring of tight muscle. I clenched, trying to resist, and he squeezed my bottom.

"No, no. This is going in. We do not want to hurt you." He kissed my bottom, his stubble tickling my sensitive skin.

"Relax, little captive." Leif stroked my hair. "You belong to us. And this is what we want. You want to please us, right?

"Yes." I turned my head to kiss his hand.

My pleasure rose, an inexorable tide I couldn't resist. Brokk tempted my climax with one hand between my legs and the other pushing the plug into my rear hole. At last, he pressed down hard and popped the wooden bulb into my stretched passage. I wiggled a little, my arsehole tightening around the foreign object, pussy weeping madly. The plug did not budge. I sighed and let my head fall to the pelts.

"There you go, lass." Leif stroked my neck. "All done, and without too much whining. Now, what?"

"Now we lock her back in her belt. Enjoy the mead and have her serve us while she stews a bit."

"No!" I reared up, and Brokk caught me. Chuckling, he pulled me into his lap, one hand still between my legs, his other gripping my breasts. "No? Is it your place to order us?" He swatted one breast and then the other. Light, playful slaps, hard enough to make them throb with desire.

My mouth fell open, my lips working, but no sound came out. My climax hovered out of reach. The plug pressed into my ass as I sat on Brokk's firm thigh, and when I tried to struggle away, he ground my bottom down against him, filling me. My empty cunny wept.

"Soon you'll be filled by both of us. Would you like that? Look at Leif and tell him."

"Yes," I moaned. Leif had his cock out now, stroking it slowly as he watched Brokk restrain my writhing hips.

"We will both claim you. I will take one end and Leif will take the other. We will fuck you between us and fill you with our seed. Then we'll put you back in the belt, needy and wanting. You will clean our cocks with your mouth and savor our pleasure as your own."

It was so dirty, so wrong, yet my orgasm rose faster than I could stop it. His fingers played in my throbbing folds.

"Would you like that, Willow? We'll care for you, wash you and dress you, and braid your hair. We'll keep you safe, but every day you will ache, and every night you will open your body to us. You'll remain forever a captive to our desires."

A scream tore from my mouth, a wild, keening sound echoing around the keep. Pleasure rode through my body, shaking it like a tree in a storm. Only Brokk's strong arms grounded me.

A sharp cry from Leif told me he'd taken his release. His seed spurted to the ground and set me flying again. Brokk's hand on my cunt, hard chest at my back, and lips at my ear kept me safe on earth, each touch driving pleasure deeper, rooting it in my very soul.

"Oh, Willow, Willow, Willow." Brokk raised his wet fingers to my mouth. With a little mew, I cleaned my musk off his fingers. He turned my head to him with a fist in my hair, and crushed my mouth against his. His fervent voice and touch sent aftershocks coursing through me. I drank deeply of his fierce desire, a tree coming out of drought, finding endless waters to sate her thirst. And when he finished plundering my mouth, he pressed his forehead against mine.

"We will not take you tonight, but soon. You will be ready for us."

∼

THEY DID AS THEY SAID, and more. Put me in the metal belt, made me fetch them mead, catching me in their arms and giving me sips from their cups before setting me on my knees to suckle them.

They both smiled, relaxed, almost jovial together.

As the moon reached her zenith, Leif gathered me up. In his arms, I sank into sleep like falling into deep water. The men murmured to each other, laughing, fighting no longer.

I dreamt I stood on the lake and stepped across the water. Did I walk? Did I fly? I was a white-winged bird, fleeing across the black expanse to shelter on the island. When I landed there, I was not alone.

Under the willow tree, a woman sat dressed in white, her black hair tumbling down her back. She seemed familiar. Her face was young, but her eyes were timeless.

She beckoned to me. As I came near the her pale face and tilt of her head reminded me of the statue I'd prayed to for long hours at the abbey.

My legs trembled, but she lifted a hand, the small smile on her face calming me.

When I stood beside her, we both leaned over the pool at our feet. The reflection caught my eye. Images flickered across the surface. Brokk stood on a mountaintop, mist swirling around him. In the shadows, Leif leaned against the castle wall, his eyes glowing and limbs covered with the black fur of a monster.

When I reached out to touch the water, the images swirled away, leaving nothing but the reflection of the moon.

And I realized I did not fear my heat anymore.

∽

I BLINKED, coming out of the dream.

"The moon," I said. "It's full."

Brokk and Leif fell silent. The two had been talking, laughing, joking, instead of fighting. I'd prayed for peace, and the goddess had answered.

My thoughts blurred a moment, mingling with my dream. I remembered what I saw in the reflection of the pool under the willow. I'd seen Brokk standing on the mountain, alone. Leif in the shadows, lurking as he fought the monster. One alone, one on the edge. Me in the middle. Somehow, I was the answer.

"Are you all right?" one of them asked.

I rose. Slowly, I lifted the hem of my shift and let the garment drop. Both men were standing by the time it hit the ground.

"Willow," Brokk rasped. "You don't have to do this."

"I want to." Naked, I stepped forward. "I want to please you."

"The moon bends your mind." Leif glanced at the sky.

"I do not care about the moon." I swayed my hips as I walked. "All I want is before me."

I licked my full lips, caressed my breasts. My fingers

palmed the pale orbs until they tingled. I pinched my nipples.

"Stop," Brokk's voice rang out. "Those are not yours. Only we can give you permission to touch."

I cocked my head to the side. "Well, then," I purred. "Do I have permission?"

BROKK

What do you think? Leif asked me. My whole body tensed, straining to go to hers. I knew he felt the same.

How's your control?

Good, Leif said. *But it may not last long.*

"Go to the furs," I ordered Willow. "Touch yourself, as you did last night."

"You may not climax," Leif reminded her.

She pouted a little but nodded and went to her place, her bottom jiggling as she walked. My cock jumped in my breeches.

"Our little captive is a wanton," Leif observed.

"She's everything we need." But, inside, I felt cold. Could I do this? Could we mark her forever?

Willow lay on the pelts, her legs spread, her hand running up and down her plump pink lower lips. They would be soft and silky to the touch, like rose petals. She teased her pleasure nub with one finger then let out a sexy little moan. And I made my decision.

"All fours. Hands and knees." I knelt before her and

freed my cock as she scrambled into place. "We will not be gentle," I warned.

She licked her lips, once, and opened her mouth wide enough to engulf me. She sucked until her cheeks hollowed. My muscles knotted up as I willed myself to hold back from thrusting hard into her mouth.

Leif knelt behind her. Palming her wet folds, he found her sensitive spots and teased them without mercy. She moaned around my cock as he sent her over the edge.

"Perfect," I said, and thrust my hips, fucking her face while Leif fingered her to the edge again. Her whimpers escaped around my cock as Leif set himself at the entrance to her virgin cunt.

I drew my cock out and caught her chin. "Brace yourself, lass." She nodded.

Leif groaned as he sank in. "So tight."

"Good lass," I told her. "You may take your pleasure as often as you wish this night." Leaning down, I pecked her lips. She turned it into a full-blown kiss. Angled her head and sucked on my fingers when I drew away.

"Please," she breathed, begging me. I would've fallen had I not already been on my knees. She wanted me as much as Leif. She wanted me. There was no mistaking the look in her eyes.

Leif pushed in and out of her slowly. With one last kiss, I guided her mouth over my cock again.

"Ready?" I asked Leif.

Together, we fucked her, rocking in and out, back and forth in perfect synchronization. Droplets of sweat beaded on her back. I brushed them away.

"So hot, so ready for us," Leif grunted.

Our rhythm sped up. We pounded her harder until I grew close. Pleasure flashed through me. Everything tightened as I prepared to shoot my seed into her mouth. Leif slapped her right haunch and then the other. She whimpered around my cock, and I almost lost it. "Odin's balls," I gasped.

Leif laughed. He caught her hips and finished with a series of thrusts. A second later, she went over again, moaning. I popped out of her mouth and spurted onto her face. Catching her chin, I kissed her again, tasting myself on her lips.

She panted, sagging to the pelts.

"Oh no," Leif said and drew her hips up so her bottom strained towards the sky. He bent down to put his mouth on her. The night had just begun.

∽

WE ATE and sucked her until dawn. When the moon fled and the morning star came out, Willow slept between us.

"It's begun," Leif said, passing me the mead.

I nodded. We'd waited over a century for this night, and now the day dawned on the rest of our lives. Would her love for us last?

"Oh no." He shook his finger at me. "Stone Face, do not sulk."

She roused. "Are you fighting again?

"No," I bit out. "Come, let us wash you."

"I want to sleep." She burrowed back into the furs.

I lifted her, pelts and all, and strode down to the lake. She shrieked when I tossed her in, and came up glaring.

Leif laughed until I tackled him. We wrestled on the beach. He got me knee-deep into the water before I threw him in.

Then both Leif and Willow jumped me. I dared not

fight, for fear of knocking Willow over, and this time they dunked me. She wrapped herself around me. Willow clung to my back as I swam about. I dove and watched her swim away, her hair spread out in a black web.

The afternoon passed as if a dream.

"What would you like more than anything, lass?" Leif asked we sat on top of the wall. She remained naked by our request, hair drying. I combed it with my fingers and braided it. I loved touching her.

I remember when you would not touch her. Leif raised a brow at me. I'd left my mind open to him. I ignored his comment but didn't close our bond.

"Well, Willow?" I raised a brow. "Tell us your heart's desire."

"To make sure my friends are safe."

"They are. I promise this. We will go to the mountain soon and see them."

"Why do we wait?"

"There is one thing we wish to do before we leave." I lifted the hair off her shoulder and touched the spot where we would mark her. "It will happen soon enough."

"Is there anything else you wish for? Meat, fish, an apple, cheese?" Leif ticked off his fingers.

"Somebody's hungry." She laughed, but then grew sober. "There was a girl in the orphanage. A friend. Her name was Hazel."

Hazel. The name is familiar, Leif said.

Yes. She is Knut's mate. Out loud, I told Willow, "Hazel is well. One of our warriors rescued her outside the Corpse King's cave. She accepted our friend Knut as her mate."

Willow blinked at me, her chest rising and falling rapidly.

"We should've told you earlier. She was going to send

word to you, so you'd know we were coming, but the Corpse King grew strong, and we had only a few days to take the abbey."

"Hazel's alive?" Willow repeated as if she hadn't heard anything else I'd said.

"And happy," Leif soothed. "She's at the mountain with her mate."

She shook her head, tears in her eyes.

"Odin's breath," I muttered. "Come here, lass, before you fall off the wall." I pulled her into my arms. She hugged me tight.

"Thank you," she said. "Thank you."

"The Berserkers will watch over all your friends, Willow, just as we watch over you."

⁓

WE MUST MATE and mark her, soon. Leif told me as the sun grew low in the sky. *I feel my beast. I am at the edge of my control.*

Very well. I ignored the anxiety stirring within. Leif was right. Better to claim her now, before it was too late.

You agree? Leif sounded surprised, and relieved.

She is the one for us. I said, and meant it. I'd fallen in love with Willow. I'd lost my heart when I first saw her on the road. She had frowned when we sandwiched her between us, but the air had filled with the tang of her arousal.

I swallowed hard. Love had crept up on me, sneaking past my defenses. It was almost strong enough to make me forget my old pain.

Almost.

I felt relief when my warrior brother went to get firewood, leaving Willow and I alone. Not for the first time, I cursed the brother bond. I had grown used to it over the years, but Willow made me remember my hate anew. Leif told me we would share her, but, in the past, when I shared, he took what was mine.

"The moon will be full again tonight," I commented.

"It's waning," she corrected.

"Close enough." I lifted her, loving the feel of her soft, small body against mine. She trailed her hands down my arms, testing the smooth muscle, detouring to study a scar. I held my breath as her fingers found their way to my face, tracing my square jaw and heavy brows. I wasn't a handsome man, but she touched me with the same reverence she had given Leif until I leaned in and kissed her.

When my lips left hers, she wound her arms around me with a sigh.

"Happy?" I asked her.

"I..." She hesitated. "Yes, I am. Are you?"

I grunted. "I would stay here forever, if it were safe." Whenever Leif went off to hunt, I'd pretend Willow belonged to me, and me alone.

She frowned, and seemed to pick up on my thoughts. "Why do you fight with Leif?"

"What?"

"At first I thought you did not like me, but it is him you do not like."

"You shouldn't say such things." I tried to brush her off, but she kept her arms locked around my neck.

"Why not?"

"It happened a long time ago, lass. It's nothing."

She snorted.

I stood and set her down. She let me go but followed when I took a few steps away from her. "I do not wish to speak of old wounds."

"It has not healed," she said softly.

"Very well." Red roses grew along the castle wall. I plucked a few and handed her one. The rest I ripped apart, petal by petal.

"Before I turned into a beast, I loved a woman," I said. "We planned to marry, but I put her off when I became a Berserker, for though I had great control over my beast, I would not risk her life. She also had an eye for Leif, as every woman does." I tried and failed to keep bitterness from my tone.

"Once night, she convinced me to share her. I did not want to, but I would do anything to make her happy. She told me nothing would break her love for me. I watched them together..." My throat closed. I could not say anymore.

Willow came and threaded her arm through mine.

"Brokk, you are so alone. I know what it is like to be alone."

I cleared my throat. "I will tell you the rest. One night I came back to my lodge, and she and Leif were lying together."

"What did you do?"

"What could I do? I left."

"You always leave," Leif called, coming around the curved stone wall.

I whirled to face him, hating that he'd snuck up on me. I wanted to know how much he'd heard, but I would not touch his mind to find out.

"And you always lie," I said. "I left because confronting you would call out your beast. I challenged you later, and you placed the blame on her. You were lucky I have so much control. If I hadn't, we would've fought, and the Alphas would've killed us."

"I did not—"

"Silence! I have born the burden of your beast all these years, as well as mine. I despise you," I spat the words. "You are a coward."

Leif's face darkened. His skin rippled as if he might Change. "Careful, brother."

"I am not your brother. The bond we share? I wish it didn't exist."

"Brokk," Willow said. Her small hands tugged on my arm.

I ignored her. "I should've let you die. That would've been justice."

"No," Willow gasped in horror. "Brokk, you don't mean it."

"I do."

"Please." She reached for me.

"Go to him," I pushed her away. She staggered at the force, and Leif caught her.

"What is the matter with you?" he snarled.

Shock glazed our woman's features. I'd never lost my temper with her; I always had control. I felt ashamed.

"You will be happy with him," I told Willow and left.

˜

I HEADED for the mountain but then detoured and wandered without purpose until I came to the field of wildflowers.

I remembered it like it was yesterday, the battle that forged the bond. I'd been angry, eager to do battle. While I fought, surrounded by many men, a spear had arched towards me. It would've found its mark in my heart had not Leif flung out his shield and struck it off course. He'd winked at me, and I'd growled, not in thanks, but annoyance. I owed him a debt of honor and, a few hours later, I would pay.

We fought as mercenaries, serving the Northland kings who claimed the islands far north. The opposing force could not stand before us, but they had a giant, a man with great strength. He was no match for Berserkers, but they sent him along with many other warriors against our smaller band. They cast nets over Leif and trapped him. Leif fought not to lose control. In the last battle, five warriors had not been able to regain their minds. The Alphas had stopped their rampage—by ripping the warriors' hearts from their chests. Only a Berserker can kill a Berserker.

I'd watched as the giant snared Leif and fought to his side. As the giant's axe swung down, I blocked the blow. Leif's sword ripped through the net and took the giant's head. He'd saved my life. I'd saved his. The bond formed, linking us forever. My enemy, my comrade in arms whom I despised, now could reach into my mind.

Brokk, come back. The cry came so faint, it could have been an echo, my own mind trying to tempt me. *Brokk, please. We need you. We cannot survive without you.* Lies, all lies.

I roamed over the heather-covered slopes, and Leif's call faded away. I could run back to the cliffs and reach out to the Alphas. I'd tell them to send me into battle again. I'd find the Grey Men and kill as many as I could before I fell. Willow would be fine with Leif. Perhaps that was why the mating bond formed between a triad—if one Berserker died, the other would care for his mate.

Brokk...no...

From the highest hill, I watched the mist closing in. I squinted. It headed for the ruined castle.

And then I knew I did not need to go and hunt the enemy. The enemy had come to us.

~

I RAN AS FAST as I could. The mist closed around me like a fist. At times, it choked me like thick smoke, but I pressed on, reaching for Leif. *Brother? Where are you? Get Willow out!*

The broken tower loomed ahead, and I heard a scream break out. Willow was in trouble.

I doubled my speed, and bounded onto the parapet in time to watch Leif attack.

Backed into a corner, Willow held a branch she'd plucked from the fire. She screamed again, waving her fiery weapon at the monster Leif had become.

"No, Leif!" I bellowed as he advanced on Willow. I opened the bond between us. *Do not lose control. Not now. We have waited so long.*

Cowering, Willow shook her makeshift torch at the monster, and Leif swiped the stick out of her hand, his claws extended to rake down her defenseless flesh. I tackled him, the force carrying him across the yard. We both ended up rolling, snarling. The very air around us crackled as I fought Leif, and the Change. The mist seeped into every corner, covering the keep with a thick blanket. The Corpse King's spells controlled the very weather.

"Willow," I shouted as I faced down my warrior brother, nothing but madness burning in his golden eyes.

Leif's claws swiped at me, and caught my shoulder, leaving great bloody furrows along my arm. I roared in pain, and the beast took hold.

WILLOW

I cowered against the wall, pressing into the stones so hard my spine hurt.

"Go!" Brokk ordered, but I could not move. He ducked and wove, fending Leif off. I cried out as the black beast that had been Leif rushed Brokk, who fell to his back before him. Brokk's powerful legs kicked up, sending Leif flying into the thick fog, out of sight.

"The mist," Brokk shouted. "It is the Corpse King's making. It attacks the mind." His human face disappeared, jaw elongating, fur covering his skin as he turned into a monster. "The beast," he barked. "Run."

Leif's growl echoed around the keep. I whirled and ran, ignoring the agonized snarl of a predator missing its prey.

I disobeyed and paused to glance back. On the castle wall, two men stood locked in combat as the mist swirled around them. They were equally tall and equally strong. Equally matched. One or both would not survive the fight.

And I would be alone. Alone as my mother had left me. Alone forever. Even if I found my way back to the abbey, I'd live among its ruins and haunt the empty village...

The Corpse King...attacks the mind. These were not my thoughts. Or if they were, the despair was of my own making. I could just as easily will it away.

My mind cleared.

Well done, Willow. The dulcet voice belonged to the Lady of the Lake. The water—it had stopped the Grey Men. Perhaps I could take shelter there.

The fog followed me, descending like a cloud from the keep. It overtook me, and I coughed as it clogged my nose and throat.

Behind me, an eerie howl rang out.

Quickly, Willow. The lake.

With new purpose I stumbled over a few bird carcasses on the sand. The mist poisoned everything it touched. Stripping off my garments, I ran into the water and plunged in.

~

THE WATER PARTED, even as it reflected the terrible events on the shore—two men, closer than brothers, fighting to kill one another. The worst had happened. They'd lost control. The Corpse King would pick off my guardians and then come for me.

I swam and swam, the mist over me, a never-ending veil. I would swim until I sank, and die like my loves. The Corpse King would not take me.

I almost cried out when my feet struck ground. I crawled onto the shore of the small island surrounded by mist—the island from my dream.

The fog didn't follow me as I stumbled onto the lichen-covered rocks. I shook with cold. I had to get warm. A hundred paces took me to the center of the island, empty but for a few trees and low bushes. I heard no birds.

I pushed through the brush and came to the circle of rocks surrounding one giant flat boulder. I staggered to it. The stone hummed under my touch like an old friend, warming me. I bent over the dimple in the rock that held a thin layer of rainwater. The liquid rippled and stirred, but, when it smoothed, I saw the woman from my dream. She looked younger, but it was her.

"Help me," I begged. "I am not strong enough to stop them."

"Who told you that?" she asked, her voice musical, melting, and oddly familiar.

"Please. They are hurting each other. Give me something to fight the fog and make them stop."

"The fog's only weapon is your mind. Clear it of everything but love, and you can triumph."

"I don't know how."

"You do, Willow. All your life you have craved this love. Do not cut yourself off from it."

The reflection clouded and cleared again. My men still fought on the beach, claws ripping at each other's skin, blood dripping from the wounds.

As I watched, Leif roared and attacked. I gasped. At the last, Brokk fell to his knees and thrust upwards. The redhead warrior stopped, mouth open in a silent cry. The beast receded as Leif met his brother's eyes. Brokk's face was a terrible mask as he faced his brother, arms outstretched in an almost embrace. He rose, and Leif sank down before him. Blood gurgled from his mouth. Brokk's claws had pierced through him, a fatal blow.

"No!" I screamed, and scrambled away from the pool. Enough hiding. I belonged with my warriors, even if only to hold Brokk as we watched Leif die.

Without a thought, I raced into the water, skidding onto

the moonlight path as if the lake was solid, like black glass. I ran straight back to shore. The mist parted before me.

The bond, Willow. Link to them.

I opened my mind. A second later, all the pain poured into me. Agony. Not Leif's. Brokk's.

Forgive me, my brother. The blunt-faced warrior knelt at his handsome comrade's side.

"You saved her." More blood bubbled out of Leif's mouth. His hair was wet with it.

I skidded to shore. "Oh no," I sobbed. Up close, Leif's wound looked so much worse. Blood soaked both men. Brokk's hands were stained dark like the heart of a rose. His claws had gone deep enough to carve Leif's heart out of his chest. What man could survive such a wound?

I threw myself to my knees, my hands over the wound. "No. No."

"I'm sorry." The corner of Leif's mouth jumped, as if he tried to smile.

"No, no, shhh," I hushed him, weeping. The mist swirled around us, blown back by an icy wind. Snow fell from a broiling sky, the strange weather fitting for a world gone mad.

Brokk. I wronged you many years ago. Leif's voice sounded in my head, though his lips did not move.

Brokk shook his head.

Your woman did not even want me. She wanted to make you jealous. That is why she seduced me. I was weak. Leif's eyes widened, and he gasped in pain.

"It's forgotten, brother. Forgiven. I resented you too long. For that, I am sorry."

Do not close your heart to love, Leif told us both. *Promise me.*

"Brother, please." Brokk knelt. "You cannot die. You will

not. The healing will begin. I have opened up to the bond... it will be enough to save you."

Keep Willow safe.

"Leif, no, stay with me." My hands were too small. I couldn't stem the flow of blood. "Help," I cried. "We need more help!"

"Well isn't this a pretty picture." A blonde woman appeared through the fog, walking briskly. She was short and ordinary-looking until she came closer. Her face was abnormally smooth and unlined, her expression fixed like a mask.

"Who are you?" Brokk snarled, and lunged towards her.

A flick of her hand, and he froze in place.

"Stay away," he roared, but couldn't seem to move.

I pushed my body over Leif's. "No."

"Come, Willow." The woman squatted next to me. "I'm here to help. Let me see the wound."

Leif's life was draining out as we spoke. There was no harm in letting her look. She could not kill him twice.

"Who are you?" I croaked.

"She is the witch, Yseult," Brokk said. All his anger had disappeared. "The Alphas sent her. Can you help him?"

"You did a good job of killing him," Yseult snapped. She shook her head with a sharp jerk. "You are the only one who can save him."

"How?" Brokk flung himself beside us.

"Give him your heart's blood. The same way you would turn him. It will strengthen the bond between you. He will use your strength to heal."

"Your chance to be free...of me." Leif grasped his arm. Brokk shook his warrior brother's weak hand off as if it weighed no more than a fly.

"And try to woo Willow without your ugly face? Next to you, I'm almost pretty."

"Quickly now," the witch warned.

I winced and half turned away as Brokk plunged his claws into his own chest.

Yseult watched intently, excitement illuminating her face. "Raise him up, let him drink." The witch licked her lips.

"Please," I begged the witch. "Don't let me lose both of them."

"You will not."

My sobs shook me. Brokk bent over Leif, one arm under the redhead, holding him as if in final embrace.

The mist seethed around us, tendrils trying to grasp us, dissipating when it touched the witch.

Finally, Yseult rose, and I shook myself, remembering to breathe. "It is done."

Brokk slumped over and rolled to his side, facing Leif.

"Is he—" I dared not finish the question.

Yseult gestured to Leif. "See for yourself."

Underneath the clotted blood, Leif's wound had closed. The injured warrior wheezed a little, but his color no longer matched the pallor of death.

"Brother," Brokk rasped. His own wound had healed. I sobbed harder at the sight of tears in his eyes.

The air seemed to thicken and still.

"Come, Willow," the witch called to me. "Leave them a moment and walk with me."

I rose also, and stilled. Hundreds of snowflakes hung suspended in the air. I touched one, and it sizzled a little as it melted. The rest drifted downwards like feathers.

Time had slowed. "Yseult...did you...?"

"I made sure Brokk saved his brother in time. It was all his doing...but for a little help. Come."

Reluctantly, I left the warriors and went with her to the edge of the lake.

"They will need you," Yseult told me. "They'll still quarrel. The Corpse King's mist only can prey on a weak mind. Your strength, and the magic in the bond, will keep them strong."

I swallowed hard, wanting to ask how I could possibly aid the warriors in such a way.

"Still," Yseult continued, "I wouldn't stay here longer than a night and a day. No more, in case the enemy sends his servants."

"Is the Corpse King near?"

"He is still bound to his tomb but growing in power. I dare not travel near his territory. He would catch me and absorb my essence. Even now, I must not linger."

"You're leaving? But what about the mist?"

"You have all you need to defeat it. Your fear, your despair powers this spell. The mist unleashed their beast because the monstrous side of them tries to protect them with its rage."

"But the beast doesn't protect them. It makes them lose control."

"Too much strength can be a weakness. You'll have to teach them how to temper their beast."

"Me?"

"There is one thing they share, one thing they cherish above anything else."

"What is that?" I wondered if she spoke of an object, something from their homeland, or a weapon of great value.

Yseult looked at me with an impatient expression. "You,

Willow. You can heal the bond between them, and the three of you will be as one."

I bit my lip.

"My work here is complete." Yseult waved a casual hand toward the keep. Leif and Brokk still lay in shadow. Brokk bent over the recovering warrior, clasping his hand with both of his.

"Thank you," I said. "I am grateful you came. But for you..." I choked and shook my head. "How did you know where to find us?"

"The Alphas sent me. But I found you through the mist when I sensed your magic."

"My magic?"

"Yes."

"It was the goddess." I told her of the woman of the island.

"That was not the goddess." She smiled, an eerie expression on her inhuman face.

"Then who was it?"

"Here." Yseult picked up a stick, and waved it over the edge of the water. Time sped up once more. The mists cleared away, fleeing into the forest.

"Look in the lake again." She pointed to the still, black water.

Frowning, I did. The wind ruffled the water, but under the ripples the image was clear. "That's her. The Lady of the Lake." I turned to Yseult, but she had disappeared.

The reflection at my feet was the woman I'd met on the island, who shared her wisdom and lent her strength. A woman with dark hair, green eyes, and great power. Me.

∽

"Willow," Brokk called. I walked to him and hovered my hand over the healing cut on his chest then turned to Leif. The warrior still lay on his back, propped on a stone, but his color had returned. His skin bore the scars of Brokk's deadly blow. I crumpled next to him. Brokk caught me, while Leif stroked my hair. They remained silent until I sat up.

"The witch is gone?"

"Yseult left, yes." I told them what she had said.

"We must flee this place soon." Leif sat up. He looked himself, other than his torn breeches and red-stained skin.

"Not so quickly, brother," Brokk said. "You must rest."

"I can travel," Leif protested, but Brokk shook his head.

"I am drained as well. Let us retreat to a safe place where we can stay the night. Besides, I wish to spend some time strengthening the bond." And he looked at me with hunger in his eye.

"Ah, yes, brother." Leif grinned, showing his fangs. "Where shall we rest for the night?"

"I know a place." I gazed across the water to the small island that had appeared out of the mist.

∼

The swim was long and cold, made slower because the warriors carried their packs clear of the water, but we emerged clean of blood. Leif stopped grumbling about the chill when I pointed out we could strip out of our clothes to dry them faster. He and Brokk seemed to like the idea of the three of us lying naked by the fire.

I liked it, too.

"Look at her, brother," Leif murmured, once the blaze roared high enough to cast a gold light over the water. "Is she not lovely?"

"She is," Brokk said. "And she is ours." He tossed another log on the fire and dusted off his hands. "Come here, Willow."

The firelight played over my breasts and the cleft of my sex as I approached. I swayed towards them, letting my hips dip and swivel with each step, drawing the warriors' eyes.

"Vixen," Brokk growled. As soon as I grew close, he grabbed me, his rough hands spanning my waist, his thumbs brushing the bottom of my heavy breasts. I waited, but he spoke no more, just bent and laid his hot mouth over my taut nipple. I fisted my hands in his hair, holding him to my chest as he warmed my flesh.

Is this what you wanted? he whispered in my mind.

"Yes," I sighed. My head fell back as his fangs scored me lightly, not deep enough to draw blood. His lips soothed the sting away. He repeated this on the other breast. Knees weak, I swayed back into a hard chest. Leif's arm curved around my waist as he supported me.

"We're going to claim you this night." His tongue touched my ear, traced the sensitive edge. *You'll beg us to fuck you, to keep you, to never let you go.*

I arched my head and sought his lips, one hand pulling Brokk to my chest, the other reaching back to pull Leif to my mouth. Leif's cock probed my bottom, making my cunt ache.

"Here, Willow." Brokk fell back onto the pelts, and I draped myself over him. Leif followed, kneeling at my back. We moved in a smooth and sinuous dance, swaying together as if we were not three bodies but one.

Brokk's fingers probed my wet heat. I wasted no time sliding onto his long, fat shaft, biting my lip and murmuring deep in my throat as he settled deep inside me.

"Good lass." Leif stroked my back.

I had no words. We needed none. Brokk and I kissed as Leif spread my silken fluid over my bottom hole. His smallest finger set me shivering, my mouth opening as the sensation became too much. Brokk studied me.

"You will take us both." He pinched my nipples, and I clenched on his cock.

"Easy." Leif steadied me, pushing me over to Brokk so he could tease the crack of my ass. "She's tight," he said to Brokk.

"She'll need to wear the plug more often, to be ready for us."

I groaned.

"And the metal belt," Brokk added.

I rocked on his cock, squeezing my inner muscles to distract him from his devious plan.

"She likes it. Don't try to tell us you don't, Willow. You just gushed all over my cock."

"Push against my fingers," Leif said. He entered me, stretching my tight pucker until I panted with the sensation. My head tossed back and forth. I couldn't think, couldn't breathe, couldn't move with the thick cock in my cunny and Leif's three fingers in my arse. When he pulled them out and replaced them with his cock, I whimpered.

"Calm," Brokk shushed me. "We will not hurt you."

My breath left in a gust. Leif pushed inside. The two cocks rubbed against my inner folds, an endless loop of sensation.

"Odin's balls," Brokk cursed.

"You all right, Willow?" Leif murmured.

My nipples pebbled painfully, my entire being throbbing with readiness. My men filled me, but I wanted more. "Fuck...me."

Leif responded with a thrust that threw me against

Brokk's chest. The warrior's arms went around me, holding me still as the redhead fucked my ass with all the fire and intensity he wished. Brokk steadied me, soothed me, cradled me close.

Fangs pricked my neck, another set at my back. With the pain, pleasure sliced through me, a fierce explosion that shook my body and set off my men. One by one, they climaxed, and their pleasure poured through me via the bond. I gasped, drowning, and came undone.

With shouts, the men filled me with their seed. We swapped pleasure back and forth, the bond white-hot as our climaxes struck like lightning.

When we finished, I touched Brokk's lips, wondering how we still existed. *Was it real?*

Yes. He kissed my fingertips. *It is real. And it is forever.*

I feel you, Willow. Leif nuzzled my sweaty neck. *I feel you and Brokk both.*

Brokk smiled.

A breeze cooled our fevered flesh, and then they began again to strengthen the bond. And when they were done, we slept under the branches of the willow tree bent over us like a mother watching over her child.

∼

FREE BOOK

Get a secret Berserker book, Bred by the Berserkers (only to the awesomesauce fans on Lee's email list)
Go here to get started… https://geni.us/BredBerserker

WANT MORE BERSERKERS?

These fierce warriors will stop at nothing to claim their mates...

The Berserker Saga

Sold to the Berserkers - – Brenna, Samuel & Daegan
Mated to the Berserkers - – Brenna, Samuel & Daegan
Bred by the Berserkers (FREE novella only available at www.leesavino.com) - – Brenna, Samuel & Daegan
Taken by the Berserkers – Sabine, Ragnvald & Maddox
Given to the Berserkers – Muriel and her mates
Claimed by the Berserkers – Fleur and her mates

Berserker Brides

Rescued by the Berserker – Hazel & Knut
Captured by the Berserkers – Willow, Leif & Brokk
Kidnapped by the Berserkers – Sage, Thorbjorn & Rolf
Bonded to the Berserkers – Laurel, Haakon & Ulf

Berserker Babies – the sisters Brenna, Sabine, Muriel, Fleur and their mates
Night of the Berserkers – the witch Yseult's story
Owned by the Berserkers – Fern, Dagg & Svein
Tamed by the Berserkers — Sorrel, Thorsteinn & Vik
Mastered by the Berserkers — Juliet, Jarl & Fenrir

Berserker Warriors

Ægir (formerly titled The Sea Wolf)
Siebold

ALSO BY LEE SAVINO

Ménage Sci Fi Romance

Draekons (Dragons in Exile) with Lili Zander (ménage alien dragons)

Crashed spaceship. Prison planet. Two big, hulking, bronzed aliens who turn into dragons. The best part? The dragons insist I'm their mate.

Paranormal romance

Bad Boy Alphas with Renee Rose (bad boy werewolves)

Never ever date a werewolf.

Sci fi romance

Draekon Rebel Force with Lili Zander

Start with Draekon Warrior

Tsenturion Warriors with Golden Angel

Start with Alien Captive

Contemporary Romance

Royal Bad Boy

I'm not falling in love with my arrogant, annoying, sex god boss. Nope. No way.

Royally Fake Fiancé

The Duke of New Arcadia has an image problem only a fiancé can fix.

And I'm the lucky lady he's chosen to play Cinderella.

Beauty & The Lumberjacks

After this logging season, I'm giving up sex. For...reasons.

Her Marine Daddy

My hot Marine hero wants me to call him daddy...

Her Dueling Daddies

Two daddies are better than one.

Innocence: dark mafia romance with Stasia Black

I'm the king of the criminal underworld. I always get what I want. And she is my obsession.

Beauty's Beast: a dark romance with Stasia Black

Years ago, Daphne's father stole from me. Now it's time for her to pay her family's debt...with her body.

ABOUT THE AUTHOR

Lee Savino is a USA today bestselling author. She's also a mom and a choco-holic. She's written a bunch of books—all of them are "smexy" romance. Smexy, as in "smart and sexy."

She hopes you liked this book.

Find her at:
www.leesavino.com

Text copyright © 2018 Lee Savino
All Rights Reserved

No part of this book may be reproduced in any form or by any electronic or mechanical means including information storage and retrieval systems, without permission in writing from the author. The only exception is by a reviewer, who may quote short excerpts in a review.

This book is a work of fiction. Names, characters, places, and incidents either are products of the author's imagination or are used fictitiously. Any resemblance to actual persons, living or dead, events, or locales is entirely coincidental.

Lightning Source UK Ltd.
Milton Keynes UK
UKHW012044290821
389674UK00002B/458

9 781648 470196